The
Tangled
Web

Also by B.J. Hoff
in Large Print:

The Captive Voice
The Penny Whistle
Storm at Daybreak

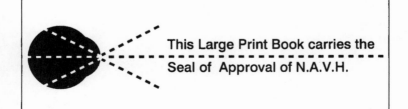

This Large Print Book carries the
Seal of Approval of N.A.V.H.

The
Tangled
Web

B.J. Hoff

Thorndike Press • Thorndike, Maine

Published in 1998 by arrangement with Tyndale House Publishers, Inc.

Thorndike Large Print ® Christian Mystery Series.

The tree indicium is a trademark of Thorndike Press.

The text of this Large Print edition is unabridged.
Other aspects of the book may vary from the original edition.

Set in 16 pt. Plantin by Minnie B. Raven.

Printed in the United States on permanent paper.

Library of Congress Cataloging in Publication Data

Hoff, B. J., 1940–
    The tangled web / B. J. Hoff.
      p.   cm.
    ISBN 0-7862-1473-2 (lg. print : hc : alk. paper)
    1. Large type books.   I. Title.
  [PS3558.034395T3   1998]
   813′ .54—dc21   98-4370

FOR JIM

Husbands are the real heroes. . . .

Like a father who untangles
What small, clumsy hands ensnare,
God unsnarls and smooths our problems
Once we trust them to his care.

B.J. Hoff
From *The Weaver*

PROLOGUE

Teddy Giordano felt his stomach wrench when he saw Nick's body slumped over the massive mahogany desk in the library. He closed his eyes and fought back a rush of tears.

Nick . . . oh, no, Nick . . .

He shuddered, forcing down the rancid taste of his own fear. He touched Nick's lifeless shoulder, then felt for a pulse at the side of his neck. Nick had been shot execution style, obviously by one of the *Family.*

Teddy yanked his hand away. *Had he suffered? Or had it been quick and painless, with death coming before he had even known what was happening?*

He dragged his eyes away from Nick's body and scanned the room. The heavy, rust-colored drapes were closed against the late afternoon light. The library was dim, illuminated only by a hand-painted desk lamp.

Only then did he realize that the telephone receiver was off the hook, its high-pitched wail insistent. He moved to pick it up, then stopped. Did he really want his fingerprints on anything in here?

He glanced down and saw the drawer of the desk standing open. Someone had had to force it — Nick always locked that drawer. Always. That was where he kept his gun . . . and, until recently, the small, black notebook.

The drawer was empty. No gun. No notebook.

Teddy hadn't expected the notebook to be there. It had already been hidden. *But what about the gun?*

He wiped his hands on his jeans, then raked his fingers through his hair. For an instant, his shock at finding Nick dead was replaced by an unexpectedly powerful wave of grief. The man slumped over the desk had been his boss — no, more than a boss. He had been almost like a big brother to Teddy. Nick had been good to him, had cared about him.

"Stay out of the business, Teddy," Nick had often warned him. "It's not for you. You're a good kid. You shouldn't sell yourself out. Just work for me, personally. Not the Family."

Nick Angelini was the only man Teddy had ever trusted. Nick had become his family, he and the kids.

The kids!

Teddy's head snapped up sharply. *Where were the kids?*

ONE

Teddy's boots whacked the glistening wood floor as he bolted from the library. He stopped in the hall, squinting up the dark stairway.

"Nicky?" His voice echoed in the high-ceilinged entrance hall. "Stacey? You up there?"

As he stood there, listening, his mind replayed his earlier conversation with Nick. At the time, he hadn't realized it would be their *last* conversation. . . .

"They're going to hit me, Teddy. At least, they're going to try. I violated the *omerta,* the code of honor. They know about the notebook, that I'm going to turn it in and testify against Sabas." His dark eyes raked Teddy's face, studying him closely. "I hate to do this to you, *compagno.* But I've got no one else. You have to take the notebook and the kids, Teddy."

Teddy backed away from Nick, shaking his head. "Uh-uh. No way. I'm a driver, a gofer, not a hero."

"You're more than that, and you know it," Nick said with soft rebuke. "You are *fratello mio* — my brother. You love my kids. And they love you. If they lose me, they have nobody. A dead mother they don't even remember, a dead father —"

"What about your sister?"

"My sister is a stranger to them. You're family."

"No one's going to hit you, Nick," Teddy protested. "Get out. Take the kids and leave."

"Teddy, Teddy," the older man said, shaking his head sadly, "you know better. I've betrayed the Family. There's nowhere to run. Nowhere."

"I can't do it," Teddy insisted. "I'm not like you, Nick. I drive cars, that's all. I can't take care of your kids. I have nothing to offer them. Besides, how could anyone know about the notebook, about what you're planning to do?"

Unexpectedly, the older man grabbed the front of Teddy's jacket. "Sabas is going to have me killed," he grated roughly. "The word is out. I'm a dead man. And you know as well as I do what will happen to my kids. They'll be raised by one of the other *caporegimes*. I don't want that for my kids, Teddy! I want them to grow up clean and

11

decent, not caught up in the business."

He dropped his hand away then, slapping Teddy lightly, affectionately, on the cheek. "Sorry, kid. I'm nervous today, that's all."

"What do you want me to do?" Teddy didn't even try to mask his resentment. He owed Nick. *But this much?*

"I want you to take the kids and the notebook and get out of here," Nick said. "Before tonight. I have money for you — a lot. Enough to take care of the three of you for a long time, if necessary. But you've got to go *now* — as soon as possible!"

"But *where*, Nick?"

"To Virginia. There's a man there who works for the Federal Witness Protection Program," Nick explained hurriedly. "He's been straight with me. Once you get the notebook to him, they can move on Sabas and put him out of business. For good. Everything they need is in that notebook, Teddy. Even without my testimony, they can finish him."

A shadow of hopeless resignation clouded Nick's eyes. "I'll never testify, Teddy. But you can save the evidence. And you can save my kids, if you do what I ask."

They studied each other in silence. Then Teddy nodded shortly. "I'll need a car."

"Take the limo."

"It's low on fuel. I was planning on going into town later this evening and filling it up."

"Do it now. I'll have Nora pack for the kids while you're gone."

"Nora's off today, remember?" Teddy felt a pang of sympathy for the kindhearted, elderly housekeeper. She adored both Angelini children. She would be inconsolable when she realized they were gone.

"Then Nicky can pack for both of them."

"You're coming with us, or I'm not going."

"*No!* the only chance you and the kids have is to go without me. If I go, they'll kill us all." He paused. "I can buy you a little more time by staying here."

Nick took Teddy into the library and gave him a bundle of money from the safe, more money than Teddy had ever seen. "Now get moving," Nick ordered. "I'll talk to the kids while you're gone. They'll be ready when you come back."

Still Teddy hesitated. "Nick . . ."

The older man swallowed hard, then reached out to grip Teddy's shoulder. "Thank you, *compagno.* You've been a good friend."

Some friend, Teddy thought with self-disgust as he called the kids' names once again. *I've let Nick be murdered and lost his kids, all inside of two hours.*

He bounded up the stairs, taking them two at a time, then raced down the carpeted hallway to Stacey's room. He threw open the door, only to find the pink bedroom empty.

Next he went to Nicky's room, but there was no sign of the boy.

He went on down the hall, flinging open one door after another. After checking the entire second floor and finding nothing, he ran back downstairs, charging through the enormous, drafty rooms with mounting anxiety.

Had they taken the kids?

In desperation, he hurtled down the basement steps.

"Nicky? Stacey? Are you down here?"

A soft thump sounded overhead, a few feet away. Cautiously, Teddy followed the sound.

"Stacey? Nicky? Can you hear me? It's Teddy."

A faint whimper answered him. He looked up, then raised both hands to unlatch the hook on the laundry chute.

Stacey tumbled out first, practically falling into Teddy's arms. She was crying.

Teddy tucked the little girl securely against his chest with one hand, then reached up to help her brother.

Nicky landed lightly on his feet and stood staring at Teddy, his dark eyes burning with a combination of fear and anger behind the thick-lensed, silver-framed glasses.

"What were you guys doing in the *laundry chute?*" Teddy snapped incredulously.

The chunky little girl in his arms began to cry harder, and he quickly gentled his tone, patting her helplessly on the back. "Don't cry, baby. It's all right." He gave one stubby dark pigtail a gentle tug. "Look at Mrs. Whispers," he said, pointing to the frayed rag doll Stacey was clutching tightly against her. "She isn't crying."

Teddy turned to the boy. "Are you kids OK?"

With the back of his hand, Nicky brushed a tangle of dark, ragged hair away from his forehead. "He's dead, isn't he? Papa's dead."

Teddy stared at him without answering, still cradling the sobbing little girl against his shoulder. He glanced at Stacey, then nodded curtly to the boy.

"Where were you? Did you see anything?"

Nicky swallowed, his thin neck making the reflex motion appear strangely pathetic to Teddy. "No. Papa sent us upstairs. He told us to hide if we heard anyone in the house."

The boy removed his glasses and, in a decidedly adult gesture, wiped a hand over his eyes. "Someone kept banging on the door." His voice wavered for an instant. "It was quiet for a few minutes. Then we heard a shot."

Teddy moistened his lips and glanced from Nicky to the weeping little girl in his arms. He wished he could think of something to say. He wished he could *think*.

"Papa said you were going to take us somewhere," the boy went on in an odd, flat tone of voice. "He told me to pack a suitcase for both of us. Are we still going to leave?"

Teddy nodded. "Yeah. Right now. You got your stuff together?"

"In the kitchen."

"Let's go." Still holding Stacey in his arms, Teddy turned and started up the basement stairs.

When they reached the hallway, he glanced toward the open library door.

The boy started toward the room.

"Don't go in there, Nicky!" Teddy cautioned sharply. "Get your coats, both of you. We have to get out of here."

Nicky looked at him, then at the open door, hesitating.

"Don't, Nicky," Teddy repeated tersely.

The boy continued to stare toward the library for another moment, then crossed the hall and opened the closet door.

Teddy set Stacey on her feet and took her hand. "Come on, baby. Let's get you into your coat."

Quickly, he zipped up his own jacket, then helped Stacey into her red parka. "That's my good girl," he said softly, managing a smile as he straightened.

She was no longer crying, but her dark brown eyes were large and solemn. "Nicky said we can't see Papa anymore, that he isn't going with us." Her small voice sounded frightened and much younger than her six years. "Mrs. Whispers is going with us, isn't she?"

"Anywhere you go, Mrs. Whispers goes, sweetheart," Teddy assured her with a hug.

In the kitchen, Teddy looked out the window, then cracked the door connecting to the garage, peering into the dimness.

A thought struck him, and he twisted his mouth to one side impatiently. "You kids wait here a minute. I have to make a quick call before we go."

Teddy returned to the library, resolutely

averting his eyes from Nick's body. His hand shook as he dug a handkerchief out of his back pocket and used it to pick up the receiver. He pressed the button to clear the line and get a dial tone, then called Frank Vincent, Nick's lawyer.

Disguising his voice, Teddy hurriedly advised Vincent of Nick's murder. Then he fled the room, not looking back.

In the kitchen, he picked up Stacey's suitcase, started to open the door to the garage, then turned to Nicky. If Nick's death was not to be a total waste, Teddy had to be sure about the notebook. "There's a book," he said. "One of those little pocket jobs. It was important to your papa —"

Before he could finish, Nicky nodded. "I know all about it. Don't worry — it's safe."

Teddy heaved a sigh of relief. "Get your stuff and come on," he said, gesturing toward Nicky's suitcase. He wished he'd had time to pack a few things for himself.

Teddy hurried them into the garage, fumbling for his keys as he went. If only they could get out of here without being seen, maybe they had a chance.

Nicky lifted his suitcase into the silver limousine's large trunk. "Where are we going?"

Without answering, Teddy hustled both

children into the front seat, then ran around the car and got in on the driver's side. He pressed the power door-locks and gunned the engine to life. As soon as the garage door went up, he backed out of the garage, tires squealing.

"Where are we going, Teddy?" the boy asked again.

Teddy righted the limo, glancing in the rearview mirror as the car surged forward. "On a long trip," he finally said. "I'm taking you to a place your papa told me about."

Without looking at him, Nicky replied knowingly, "Where we'll be safe."

Teddy glanced over at him. "Where you'll be safe," he repeated. "That's my job now," he said softly. "Keeping you and Stacey safe."

"We can't get away from them, you know," Nicky said woodenly. "There isn't anywhere we can go that they won't find us."

Teddy knew that Nicky Angelini was one smart kid. A genius, the headmaster at that fancy private school had told Nick. An honest-to-goodness nine-year-old prodigy. At the moment, however, Teddy fervently hoped even a genius could occasionally be wrong.

TWO

East-Central West Virginia
Palm Sunday

Jennifer Kaine came awake in an instant, bolting upright in bed. She pulled the blanket up to her neck and tried to focus her eyes in the dark bedroom.

The room was thickly shadowed, unfamiliar. It was also cold. Jennifer looked down toward the iron bedstead at her feet, then across the room at the sliding glass doors.

Outside, huge pine trees and grasping maples fought each other for control of the night sky. The blackness was relieved only by a faint spray of light from the security lamp that stood a few feet away from the cabin.

The cabin.

Finally, her head cleared. They were at the Farm, not at home. She glanced over at Daniel. He was still asleep, his breathing deep and regular. Sunny, Daniel's golden retriever guide dog, also stirred restlessly from her rug beside the bed.

The digital clock on the bedside table showed almost midnight. Jennifer had been asleep for nearly an hour, exhausted from the ride to the Farm and the work they had done upon their arrival: carrying in supplies, stacking wood for the fireplace, and loading the pantry shelves. It had been eleven o'clock before she had collapsed onto the plump feather bed, every muscle in her body rioting in rebellion.

Now, fully alert, she tried to figure out what had roused her from her deep sleep. There had been a noise — a noise out of place for her surroundings. With the covers still wrapped snugly around her shoulders, she lay listening.

Suddenly, a soft thumping sound, like the muffled thud of running feet, broke the quiet. At the same time, Sunny leaped to her feet, uttering a low, warning growl.

Someone was on the deck.

A wraparound wooden deck circled the cabin, with steps descending to the yard on both sides. It sounded to Jennifer as if someone was at the far end of the cabin, near the kitchen.

Then, abruptly, there was nothing but silence — a silence so total that Jennifer could hear her own heart pounding. She stared with growing dread at the glass doors at the end of the room, half expecting to see someone stop in front of them and gape back at her.

With another perfunctory growl, Sunny went to stand in front of the doors and look out. Chilled, Jennifer reached to shake Daniel awake.

"Daniel! Daniel, wake up!" Fear made her whisper scrape like sandpaper in the hushed bedroom.

Sunny now crossed to Jennifer's side of the bed.

Daniel was slow to stir.

"Daniel!" Jennifer shook him again, harder this time. "There's someone outside!"

Finally, he pushed himself up. "What's wrong?" he said, brushing the hair out of his eyes.

"I heard something outside," Jennifer whispered. "Like . . . someone running across the deck."

The instant Sunny saw that her master was awake, she went back to his side of the bed. The retriever stood watching Daniel shake his head and yawn.

"Someone running?" he muttered. "What time is it, anyway?"

Jennifer flipped back the blankets and swung her feet over the side of the bed.

"I'm going to see what's going on," she said, grabbing her robe from a nearby rocking chair.

"Jennifer, wait a minute —"

But Jennifer wasn't about to wait. She wanted to make sure the glass doors were locked. She crept stealthily across the plank floor, flinching at the cold wood beneath her bare feet. There were no drapes at the doors, a condition Jennifer intended to remedy before sleeping another night in this room. She would use sheets or blankets if she had to.

She edged up to the glass, holding her breath as she peered outside. Nothing. The lock was secure.

After a moment, she went to the window at the other side of the room and opened a shutter. Daniel, blind for nearly six years now, shrugged into his robe and came to stand behind her. Sunny followed, wedging herself between the two of them.

"Can you see anything?" Daniel murmured, putting a hand on Jennifer's shoulder.

"Nothing." Jennifer strained for a better look, but her view was obscured by the dense grove of trees that rimmed the cabin. "It's too dark."

"How long have you been awake?"

"Just a few minutes. The noise startled me."

"You don't suppose Jason is up wandering around, do you?"

Jennifer tensed. Nine-year-old Jason, whom she and Daniel had adopted a few months ago, was mildly retarded; she continually had to fight her tendency to overprotect him. At the moment, Jason was supposed to be asleep in the loft bedroom, but Daniel's question prompted a stab of concern.

"I'd better go see. If he's up at this time of night, he must be sick."

"Wait. I'll go with you."

With Sunny following right behind them, Jennifer guided Daniel from the room with her hand in his. "I wonder if Gabe or Lyss heard anything," she whispered as they made their way through the darkened great room toward the stairway.

"I hope not. If Gabe wakes up, we're all up for the night," Daniel muttered. "It only takes a couple hours of sleep to charge him for the next day. He'll yak till dawn if he gets up now."

Gabe Denton and Daniel were as close as brothers. Not only had they been best friends for years, but Gabe also managed the radio station Daniel owned — and had recently married Daniel's sister, Lyss. The newlyweds had come along this week to help get the Farm ready for its first visitors of the year, weekend campers who would begin to arrive the week after Easter.

For the last four years, Daniel and Gabe, as well as others from the church, had worked to convert what had once been a family-owned farm into a Christian summer camp for disabled children. This year, the two couples had offered to fill in for the overworked, year-round supervisor and his wife while the couple took a brief vacation before the summer camping season.

Jennifer's mind raced through all the possibilities as she hurried upstairs, leaving Daniel and Sunny below. She found Jason sleeping soundly in the enormous old four-poster that had once belonged to Daniel's grandparents. She stood watching him for a moment, then tucked the bedcovers more snugly around him and went back downstairs.

"Well, it wasn't Jason I heard," she told Daniel. "I don't think he's moved since we tucked him in." She paused. "Daniel, maybe we ought to wake Gabe and have him look around outside."

"It was probably just a wild dog, Jennifer. Let's go back to bed." He turned and would

25

have started out of the room if Jennifer hadn't stopped him.

"A *wild dog?*" she repeated, clutching his arm.

He nodded. "We get them all the time out here. People dump them out on the highway, and they come around looking for food."

Jennifer's stomach knotted at the thought of stray dogs circling the cabin in the middle of the night. Still, she couldn't buy Daniel's explanation.

"That was no dog," she said stubbornly. "Not unless he was wearing shoes."

Daniel sighed. "Whatever you heard, darlin'," he said reasonably, "is gone now. Come on — let's get some sleep." He covered her hand on his arm and started toward the bedroom.

But he moved a little too fast for Jennifer, and she crashed into the corner of a large pine table.

"Ohhh, Daniel! My *toe!*"

Daniel caught her around the waist.

"What happened?"

"My toe!" Jennifer wailed. "I think I broke my toe!"

"How?"

"*How?*" Jennifer stared at him. "I ran into a table, that's how! It's pitch black in here."

Daniel pulled her to him and began to pat her back, much as he might have tried to comfort Jason. "But why?"

"Why *what?*" Jennifer's eyes smarted with tears of pain and exasperation.

"Why is it dark in here? Why didn't you turn on the lights? Just because I have to navigate in the dark doesn't mean *you* do."

At that moment the lights went on. Jennifer jerked in surprise, but it was only Gabe. Gabe, in a Chinese red monk's robe trimmed in gold satin. Directly behind him, peering over his shoulder with eyes that were little more than slits, stood Lyss. She looked lost and somehow forlorn in an oversized bathrobe that bore a strong resemblance to a horse blanket.

Gabe studied them, his hand still poised on the light switch. "What's going on?" he grumbled, flipping a shock of sun-streaked blond hair out of his eyes. "What are you guys doing out here in the dark?"

"We were looking for a wild dog wearing shoes," Daniel said mildly. "But Jennifer — who apparently *isn't* wearing shoes — stubbed her toe. Will one of you take a look at it?"

Gabe studied Daniel for only a moment before giving a shrug and crossing the room. He helped Jennifer to the well-worn chintz chair by the fireplace, steadying her as she sat down.

Lyss watched them with a vacant stare and an enormous yawn. After another moment, she moved to help. "I don't think it's broken, Jennifer," she said as she examined the throbbing toe.

"Well, it *feels* broken," Jennifer muttered.

Behind Lyss, Gabe rolled his eyes and shrugged again. "So what were you doing, anyway? It's after midnight."

Daniel explained while Lyss went to make an ice pack for the toe.

"Probably a 'coon," Gabe said mildly. "Or maybe a stray dog."

Jennifer gritted her teeth. "If you don't mind," she grated, "I don't want to hear anything else tonight about stray dogs."

She saw Daniel barely suppress a grin, but his expression appeared convincingly sober when he spoke. "Why don't we help you back to bed, darlin'?" he said. "You can take the ice pack with you."

At that point Gabe offered to make coffee for everyone — "as long as we're all awake anyway."

Daniel grimaced, but it was Lyss who answered. "Some of us," she told her husband with a bleary-eyed glare, "are *not* awake. Nor do we want to be. At least not for another eight hours."

Soon the cabin was again dark and quiet. Daniel had already turned over to go back to sleep, but Jennifer wasn't ready to let it go — not yet. "I *did* hear something, Daniel," she insisted, her voice hushed. "And it wasn't a dog."

She waited, but there was no reply except from Sunny, who whimpered sympathetically from her side of the bed.

THREE

As the limousine slowed, then came to a stop, Chuck Arno roused from sleep and sat up in the backseat, grumbling. Boone, the stoop-shouldered driver hunched behind the wheel, glanced nervously in the rearview mirror, then at the passenger beside him. He started to speak, stopped, cleared his throat, and tried again.

"How much longer are we gonna keep lookin', Wolf?" Boone's voice was reedy, almost whining.

In the passenger's seat, Wolf looked at Boone. Arno could see his frigid blue eyes in the mirror as Wolf studied Boone for a moment. Finally, without answering the question, he turned his gaze back to the road. Pressing his index finger to one side of his nose, he sniffed, once, then again — a habit that never failed to irritate Arno.

"Where are we?" he muttered, leaning over the front seat. "Why'd you stop, Boone?" He wiped a hand across his eyes, forcing himself awake, then stretched to look at himself in the rearview mirror. Arno

30

grimaced at his own reflection — an overweight middle-aged man with swarthy skin and dark eyes, now red-rimmed and bloodshot. Automatically, his mind snapped shut, denying what he saw. He looked away.

"Got to get some gas," the driver snapped. "Hard to tell where we'll find another station this time of night, out here in the sticks."

Wolf, a small, wiry man with the coldest eyes Arno had ever seen, finally spoke. "We should give the Boss a quick call. He'll be wondering what's going on."

"You call, Wolf," the driver wheedled. "You know he's gonna be mad."

Wolf picked up the cellular phone from the seat beside him and flipped it open. He listened for a second, then closed the phone again. "We're too far out of range. Use the pay phone at the gas station." He eyed Boone suspiciously. "Why would P.J. be mad, Boone?"

Boone killed the engine but continued to stare straight ahead. His large, gnarled hands were none too steady on the steering wheel.

From the back seat, Arno watched the driver squirm, mildly amused at his discomfort. It was a common joke that Boone Scavarelli spent half of his life being scared

31

to death of the Boss — P. J. Sabas — and the other half being terrified of Wolf.

When Boone glanced back at him, as if looking for support, Arno felt a familiar sting of impatience. The man's wandering eye was an imperfection that grated on him. He could never quite tell where Boone was looking. Worse, Arno thought with distaste, the man was a bumbler — none too bright. For the life of him, he couldn't figure why Wolf insisted on taking old Boone along wherever they went.

The aging driver was still pleading with Wolf. "He'll likely think we should have caught up with them by now."

"P.J.'s a patient man," Wolf answered with another sniff. "Just tell him we're closing in."

"Closing in?" Boone looked at him incredulously.

Wolf smiled at him. In the backseat, Arno moistened his lips, fidgeting as he watched the two.

Jay Wolf was neither ugly nor good-looking. At first glance, he might have been labeled ordinary, with his acne-scarred complexion, his small, narrow-shouldered frame, and his limp, light-brown hair. But when he smiled, his appearance underwent a startling transformation. His lips opened on a wide mouth that was overcrowded with surprisingly large teeth, some of which tapered to fanglike points. At the same time, his pale eyes narrowed menacingly, making his surname, "Wolf," eerily appropriate.

Still smiling broadly, he nodded. "That's what I said, Boone. Closing in."

"But, Wolf, we ain't got a thought where they —"

The smile disappeared. "Here's how I see it, Boone," said Wolf, casually resting one arm against the car door. "We've temporarily lost Giordano and the kids, true. But if we cover every county road, every country lane, and every cow path, we'll eventually find them. Right?"

He paused, again smiling, as if he had generously forgiven the older man his temporary lapse of confidence. "Now, Boone, you know they can't hide a flashy silver limousine like Angelini's out here in the woods too long. It seems pretty simple to me. We find the car, we find Giordano and the kids. Even if they try to hole up somewhere, they can't ditch that limo without us finding it eventually. Isn't that right, Chuck?" He turned to look at Arno.

Caught off guard, Arno hesitated, then gushed, "Right, Wolf. That's how it looks to me."

Wolf nodded and turned around. "You see, Boone? Just tell the Boss we're closing in and things are looking good. Real good."

Without meeting his gaze, Boone pulled up the zipper of his hooded jacket and hauled himself awkwardly out of the car. He pumped his own gas, paid the attendant at the register inside, then lumbered over to the pay phone at the side of the stucco building.

"Boone's nervous," Wolf said conversationally, his eyes on the older man using the phone. "You nervous, too, Chuck?"

"Me?" Arno laughed, a little too loudly. "No way, Wolf. Nothing to be nervous about, right? It's like you said. How hard can it be to spot that limo of Nick's?"

A cold finger seemed to touch the back of his neck when Wolf half turned and smiled at him. "Boone's getting old, I'm afraid. We'll have to watch him, Chuck."

Arno quickly agreed. "Yeah. Yeah, maybe we'd better."

Wolf was still smiling when Boone returned to the car.

"So, did you talk to the Boss?"

Boone nodded, giving Wolf an anxious look. "He's burnin'. Just like I said."

Wolf shrugged. "He'll be OK. Relax, Boone. You worry too much." He touched his nose and sniffed. "Let's move."

Boone started the car and eased away from the pump. "The Boss is really upset, Wolf," he said with an uneasy glance. "You know what he told me?"

"No, Boone. What did he tell you?" Wolf smoothed the velvet lapel of his gray chesterfield.

"He said to tell you to bring Giordano and the kids back by the end of the week or not to come back at all. He said that, Wolf."

Wolf looked at him for a moment, then turned away, saying nothing.

In the back, Arno folded his arms across his chest and slouched down in the seat. Sometimes he wished he was still collecting markers. At least then he wouldn't have to spend so much time with Wolf. The guy gave him the creeps, and that was the truth. There was something weird about him, something . . . scary.

He had never met anyone like Wolf. Even the Boss — who could turn mean as a snake sometimes — wasn't strange like Wolf. At least with P.J. you always knew where you stood; you could tell when you were in trouble with him.

But not with Wolf. The guy was totally unpredictable. Icy cold most of the time, except when he had one of those fits of his. Then he turned into a crazy man, a real mental case. And you never knew when it was going to happen. He would be smiling that blood-freezing smile of his one minute, and the next thing you knew, he'd be roaring and crashing around like a rabid . . . wolf.

Arno shuddered inside his black leather jacket. When this was over, he told himself for the hundredth time, he was going to talk to the Boss about some new action. Something out of Wolf's territory.

FOUR

Monday

By dinnertime the next evening, Jennifer had decided that her sore toe might be a blessing in disguise. Her work detail for the day had been the lightest of all, and now, listening to the others rehash their efforts, she could enjoy the conversation guilt free.

Her chief duties had been to help Gabe inventory the storage pantry and give him a hand with lunch and dinner.

By mutual consent, Gabe had been appointed chef for the group. His hobby was cooking, and he approached it as he did everything else, with dizzying energy and unbounded creativity.

His menu for the evening meal was no exception, Jennifer thought as she dished up a generous second helping of Creole gumbo.

She glanced at Lyss, who sat studying the last bite of food on her plate with obvious regret. "I guess I'll forgive you for not helping us clean the cabins," Lyss told Gabe.

"This is scrumptious stuff, love." She lifted the final taste of gumbo to her mouth and took her time finishing it off.

"Save room for dessert," Gabe warned as he started scraping dishes in the sink.

Daniel pushed himself back from the harvest table with a contented sigh. "Dessert, too? What are we having?"

"Lemon mousse," Jennifer put in. "And almond cookies."

Daniel, who loved anything citrus, made a small sound of satisfaction and gave a deep stretch. "When's snack time?"

Jennifer watched out of the corner of her eye as Jason soaked up the last bite of gumbo on his plate with a piece of roll and started to put it in his mouth, then stopped. He looked at the retriever sitting next to him and then, after a furtive glance at the adults, quickly palmed the bread.

"Don't even think about it, Jason," Jennifer said warningly, eyeing the boy and the dog.

Jason studied her face. When he saw one corner of her mouth twitch, he grinned at her, as if he knew he was still on safe ground. Blinking once, he said gravely, "But Sunny hasn't had any dinner."

"Well, she's not going to have her dinner at the table," Jennifer said firmly. "You can feed her after we're done. Outside."

"But you'd better not give her any of that gumbo, Jason," Daniel told him. "It's too spicy."

"So spicy you had three helpings," Gabe countered dryly from the sink.

"I'm immune," Daniel said pleasantly. "I'm used to Jennifer's cooking."

Jennifer elbowed him. "Daniel will have gummy oatmeal for breakfast, Gabe. Nice and cold."

Gabe wiped his hands on a dish towel, then returned to the table. "My count in the storage pantry didn't tally, Dan," he said, scooting onto the bench across from Daniel. "Either Mac's first count was wrong, or there's some stuff missing."

"What kind of stuff?" Daniel crossed his arms over his chest and leaned back against the wall.

"Blankets and pillows. I was three short on each. Jennifer checked my count, just to make sure."

"Don't forget the food shelves," Jennifer reminded him. "According to the list Mac gave us, there should be two large jars of peanut butter in addition to what we counted. Plus three bags of marshmallows and two boxes of crackers."

Daniel leaned forward, drained the milk

from his glass, then dabbed his mustache with his napkin. "Mac is as accurate as a CPA with that storage pantry," he said, getting up to take his dishes over to the sink. "Maybe some things just got misplaced."

Gabe shook his head. "Nope. We checked every likely place. His gaze swept the room. "Who's up for the dishes tonight?"

When a long silence greeted his question, he shrugged. "OK. Who wants to get up at six tomorrow morning and cook breakfast?"

"Jennifer and I will take care of the dishes," Daniel quickly offered, pushing up his sleeves. "You just sit down and enjoy your coffee."

Gabe smiled at Lyss and Jennifer. "Cooperation. That's what makes this team *work*."

Later, Jennifer sat on the overstuffed sofa in the great room, looking around. She loved this room — mostly because it was so *friendly*. The huge stone fireplace was the focal point of the entire room. A fire burned there anytime the mercury dipped low enough. The furniture was big, worn, and comfortable. Jennifer had come to think of the cabin as a second home, and this particular room as the heart of that home. It was a happy room, she often thought, a good-natured, smiling kind of room where people could be themselves and enjoy each other.

She looked across the room to see Daniel retrieving his old Martin flattop guitar from the corner. Lyss went hunting for her banjo, and soon they were singing camp choruses.

After a time of prayer together, Daniel got up and put his guitar away. "I'm ready for dessert."

"We'll get it," Gabe said, pulling Lyss up from the couch with him. "It's in hiding. You don't leave dessert within reach of Dan the Dumpster."

When they came back, Gabe was empty-handed and scowling. "OK, so you found the cookies, Kaine. Are there any left?"

Daniel, standing with his face toward the fire, turned with a puzzled frown. "What?"

"The cookies, Daniel," Gabe repeated with forced patience. "Where are the cookies?"

Lyss followed her husband into the room, laughing at his aggravation. "Better 'fess up, Dan. He's just stubborn enough to lock up the mousse if you don't share the cookies."

"What are you two talking about? I don't know anything about the cookies."

Jennifer thought Daniel's expression looked entirely genuine, but she could never

41

be sure. "Gabe, you said you made two dozen. Even Daniel can't eat that many cookies in an afternoon."

They went on arguing for another few minutes, Gabe insisting that his brother-in-law was the only conceivable suspect, while Daniel's injured look of denial became more and more convincing.

"I've got it!" Jennifer exclaimed finally, her smile saccharine. "I'll bet it was that wild dog you fellows told me about last night."

Gabe shot her a disgusted look.

"I bet I know who took the cookies."

All four adults stopped talking and turned to look at Jason.

From his place on the hearth rug beside Sunny, the boy pushed a strand of straight blond hair away from his eyes. "Probably it was the children in the woods."

No one said anything for a moment. "What are you talking about, Jason?" Jennifer finally asked.

He looked up at her and smiled. "I saw them today, when I took Sunny outside. While Daddy and Aunt Lyss were cleaning the cabin. A boy and a girl. I think they want to be my friends."

"Jason," Daniel said patiently, "didn't we just have a talk a few days ago about make-believe friends? I thought you were going to stop pretending."

The boy shook his head. "But these aren't pretend friends, Daddy. They're real."

Daniel frowned. "Jason —"

As if wounded by the unfamiliar note of irritation in his father's voice, Jason suddenly stopped smiling and fastened his wide brown eyes on Daniel. "They *are* real."

"Jason, *you* didn't take the cookies, did you?" Daniel asked, his tone sharp.

"No, sir." The boy's crestfallen expression reflected dismay that Daniel would even ask.

During the somewhat awkward silence that followed, Gabe and Lyss discreetly left the room. After a moment, Jennifer said, "Jason, these . . . children . . . where exactly did you see them?"

"Jennifer!" Dan's expression darkened.

"Wait, Daniel — please. Let him tell us."

"They came from behind the tree." Jason watched Jennifer's face carefully.

"What tree, honey?" she pressed.

"The big one, at the end of the gate."

"What did they look like?"

He thought for a moment. "The boy has black hair, like Daddy's. And big glasses."

"You said there was a girl, too?" Jennifer prompted gently.

Jason nodded. "She has tails that stick out, like this." He raised both hands to his ears and made a pulling motion.

"Pigtails? Is that what you mean?"

Again, he nodded. "She's little," he said in a condescending tone. "And round."

"Round?" Jennifer repeated.

"Not like you. She's —" He made the shape of a ball with his hands. "Round."

"Jennifer, do you really think we should encourage this?" Daniel asked shortly.

Jennifer studied him, surprised at the annoyance etched on his face. Finally, she turned back to Jason. "Why don't you go up and get ready for bed, honey. We can talk more about this in the morning. All right?"

Jason gave her an unexpectedly wise look, as if he knew no one believed him. He rubbed Sunny's ears once more, then got up. "Can Sunny go with me? Just for a while?"

Jennifer nodded. "But she has to come back downstairs soon. Daddy might need her."

The instant Jason and Sunny were out of earshot, Daniel turned to Jennifer. "You know I've been talking with him about these imaginary playmates."

Jennifer bit her lip and nodded. "Yes, I

know. But I'm not sure I understand why it bothers you so much."

"Because sometimes he carries it too far." He shoved his hands into his pockets and turned away, saying nothing more.

Puzzled, Jennifer stared at his broad back. "Daniel? Don't you think you might be making too much of this?"

He turned back to her, his strong, dark-bearded face set in a stubborn mask. "No, I don't. But I think *you* could take it a little more seriously."

"Daniel —"

"Jason's different, Jennifer," he said, ignoring her attempt to interrupt. "He doesn't always think the way you and I do. Sometimes it's hard for him to tell the difference between what's real and what isn't. I just don't want his fantasies to become too important — or too real — to him."

Exasperation rose in Jennifer, then ebbed as she realized that her husband had been uncharacteristically touchy the past few days. "Daniel, what's wrong?" she asked carefully.

He frowned. "Wrong?"

"It isn't like you to make an issue of something so small."

He said nothing, but his chin jutted out a fraction more.

A totally irrelevant thought flitted through Jennifer's mind. Daniel suddenly appeared extremely . . . large to her. It wasn't so much his considerable height, nor the expanse of his shoulders, molded by years of strenuous training as a former Olympic swimming champion. In fact, she was seldom mindful of his size. Daniel was so gentle, so kind and tenderhearted, that it was easy to forget that he towered over her and others. His sweet and unfailing devotion to her, his consideration of her feelings — even his quiet, casual Appalachian drawl — somehow tempered his formidable size and strength.

The only time she thought much about his size at all was during a rare bout of anger — or stubbornness. Like now.

She took a deep breath. "Daniel, let's go for a walk," she said quietly.

Again he frowned. "A walk?"

"Yes. Would you like to?"

After a moment, he shrugged. "It's cold out. You sure you want to?"

"I'll get our jackets." Jennifer started for the closet, then stopped. "Do you want to take Sunny?"

"No, if you don't mind helping me."

Frustration welled up in Jennifer, but she kept her tone perfectly even. "You know I don't mind."

After getting their coats from the closet, she ducked into the kitchen to tell Gabe and Lyss where they were going.

Outside, she took Daniel's arm, waiting until he covered her hand with his own before starting to walk.

They went around the front yard, then down the narrow lane leading away from the side of the cabin. The night was cold, blanketed with damp silence. Wind bent the low-hanging branches of the maple trees and moaned through the pines scattered over the grounds.

Jennifer shivered, as much from a sudden, unbidden clutch of apprehension as from the cold. She huddled a little closer to Daniel, and he slowed his pace. "You cold?"

"I'll be OK after we walk a bit. It feels as if it's going to snow."

He nodded but said nothing.

"Daniel," Jennifer ventured, "is something bothering you? Something besides this thing with Jason?" She looked up at him, feeling a familiar tug at her heart as she studied the strength and kindness molded in his profile.

His voice was soft when he finally answered. "It isn't Jason. It's me."

He stopped, but Jennifer continued to

47

cling to his arm. "What are you talking about?"

He sighed. "I don't know. Maybe I'm just overcompensating."

"I don't understand," Jennifer said.

"Neither do I." His smile was grim. "All I know is that lately I've been feeling . . . anxious. Maybe even a little insecure . . . about being a father." He hesitated. "A *blind* father. To a mentally challenged boy."

Jennifer caught her breath in dismay. "But you're a *wonderful* father to Jason! And he absolutely adores you!"

"Oh, I know he loves me — *us*," Daniel quickly agreed. "But I still want to be sure that I'm doing what's best for him. However I can, I want to ensure a decent quality of life for Jason when he grows up." He squeezed her hand. "It's always going to be harder for him, Jennifer. I have to do everything in my power to give him as much strength and wisdom as he's going to need someday. So he can do more than just . . . survive, if the time comes when he's on his own."

Jennifer studied his face, unshed tears lodging in her throat. "Oh, Daniel . . . don't you realize that Jason can't be anything *but* strong with the kind of love and caring he's going to grow up with?"

She reached up and placed her hands on either side of her husband's face, searching his sightless blue eyes. "Daniel, you're a *marvelous* father — truly, you are. And Jason is going to grow up to be a fine, strong man, in spite of his disability." She paused. "But just as your own father didn't try to limit you — even after you were blinded — you mustn't try to limit Jason either."

He rested his hands lightly on her shoulders, saying nothing.

"Daniel," she continued, still framing his face with her hands, "you told me once that your father taught you about boundaries by giving you freedom and combining it with responsibility. You said he taught you about right and wrong by letting you make some wrong choices and take the consequences of your mistakes. Remember?"

He nodded.

"And you said that you believe God teaches us in the same way," she went on, "enabling us to stretch and grow by giving us the freedom to be wrong sometimes."

Again he gave a small nod.

Jennifer dropped her hands to his shoulders. "Well, Daniel, I think that's what you have to do with Jason, too. You have to give him some freedom. And —" She hesitated. "And I think you have to give him time to be a little boy. That's an important part of growing up, after all."

They continued to stand close, unmoving, each of them clasping the other's shoulders as Daniel seemed to consider her words. Finally, a hint of a smile softened his features. "And I suppose you think Jason's make-believe friends are a part of growing up as well?"

"Yes, I do." Jennifer paused. "I had a pretend friend when I was a little girl. His name was Bob."

"Bob?" One dark eyebrow lifted.

"He was a big-brother type," Jennifer explained matter-of-factly. "Protected me from all the bullies on the block, that kind of stuff."

Daniel put his arms around her. "Somehow, love, I can't imagine you having too much trouble with bullies."

"No?"

"No. It's a lot easier to imagine you chasing the bullies away." He kissed her gently on the forehead.

"I did that, too. But only when Bob was with me."

He shook his head, then turned at the sound of voices drifting toward them from the cabin. "Are Gabe and Lyss out here, too?"

50

Jennifer turned to glance at the cabin. "They're on the deck." She smiled as she watched Gabe hold Lyss in his arms. "Acting like newlyweds."

Daniel tightened his embrace, coaxing her closer. Leaning into his strength, Jennifer smiled at how warm it always seemed to be in his arms. She tilted her face to his.

"And do *you* still feel like a newlywed, Mrs. Kaine?" he asked softly, a smile in his voice.

"As a matter of fact, I do," Jennifer murmured, reaching up with one hand to touch his bearded cheek. "Do you, Daniel?"

He pressed his lips to her temple. "Not really."

Hurt, Jennifer tried to pull away from him, but he held her, smiling at her indignation. "I feel," he whispered against her hair, "like a man who is more in love with his wife than any newlywed could ever be." His lips met hers in a gentle kiss. "I love you, Jennifer Kaine. I love you more right now, at this moment, than I've ever loved you."

"You do?"

"Absolutely." Daniel kissed her again, a kiss that took Jennifer's breath away.

"Let's leave the newlyweds out in the cold and go back inside to the fire, what do you say?"

They began to walk. "By the way," he said, "what did this . . . *Bob* fellow look like?"

"He was gorgeous."

"Thought you were just a kid."

"I was." Jennifer chuckled. "But *Bob* wasn't."

He stopped. "Someday I'm going to have the last word in one of these conversations."

"Want to bet?"

Someone was crying.

At first Jennifer thought she'd been dreaming. Still only half-awake, she reached out to touch Daniel. Her hand latched onto his pillow. He was gone.

She sat up and looked around, trying to focus in the darkness. "Daniel?"

When he didn't answer, she reached over to turn on the bedside lamp, then changed her mind.

Again came the faint, muffled cries that sounded like a child weeping, penetrating the night with a chord of anguish.

For a moment, Jennifer couldn't move. Chilled, she clutched the blanket, again whispering Daniel's name. Finally, she slipped out of bed, fumbling for her robe.

Something must be wrong with Jason.

Trembling now, she pulled on her robe,

then turned toward the window. The sound was coming from outside. But that was impossible. Jason was upstairs.

Seeing nothing from the window, she turned and went to the sliding glass doors. She had hung a sheet to serve as a makeshift drape, and now she pulled it back to look outside. The deck and surrounding yard were dark. Nothing moved.

And the crying had stopped.

Rushing across the room and out into the hall, she nearly careened into Daniel, who was coming from the great room. Instead of his robe, he was wearing jeans and a ski sweater. Sunny was with him, on her harness.

"Daniel! What's wrong?"

He found her hand and tucked it under his free arm. "I thought I heard something. Did I wake you?"

"You heard it, too?" Jennifer gripped his hand. "It sounded like a child crying. Is Jason —"

"Jason's sound asleep. That was my first thought, so Sunny and I went up to check on him. He's fine."

Jennifer's throat tightened. "Then what was it?"

He shook his head. "Must have been an animal. Maybe something's hurt outside.

I'd better go check."

Jennifer threw a coat on over her robe and went with him. They walked around in the cold darkness for nearly half an hour but found nothing. At last they gave up and went back inside. If an animal *had* been nearby, it was gone.

"At least this time you heard something, too," Jennifer said as she hung up her coat. "Do you really think it was an animal?"

"What else?" He unfastened Sunny's harness and stroked the retriever's head for a moment.

"Daniel . . ."

"Hm?"

"What if Jason *did* see someone today? What if those children weren't make-believe?"

He frowned. "Children in the woods?" He gave a small laugh. "Jennifer, it's *cold* out there. Even a runaway wouldn't be hanging around in this kind of weather."

What he said made sense. But *something* had been out there. And Jason had seemed so *certain* about those two children.

"I hope the whole week isn't going to be like this," Daniel said wearily.

"Like what?"

"I'd like to get some sleep."

"Oh." Jennifer looked at him, wishing he

felt more like talking. "Daniel . . . *could* someone be out there? In the woods?"

He sighed. "Would *you* be slinking around a youth camp in thirty-degree weather at midnight, Jennifer?" He reached for her hand. "Honey, forget it. Let's get some rest."

Reluctantly, she followed him into the bedroom. In her mind, she could still hear the mournful, heart-wrenching sound of a sobbing child. Daniel was probably right. It was a ridiculous notion to even think that a child — or an adult, for that matter — would be out there in this weather.

But an hour later, Jennifer was still awake, listening. Listening for a sound that never came.

FIVE

The next afternoon, Jason started off for the big tree at the end of the lane. "Come on, Sunny — this way." Jason glanced back to make sure the retriever was following him, then took off running.

"*Hurry!*" Jason called over his shoulder. He had to find the children before someone came looking for him. He was sure the children wouldn't come out if they saw a grown-up. He didn't know exactly *how* he knew that, but he knew.

When Daddy had agreed to let him take Sunny outside to play, he warned Jason to stay "within shouting distance." He wasn't disobeying, he told himself as he and Sunny pounded down the dirt pathway at top speed. He could hear if anyone called him. The important thing was to find the children and tell them they had to return the cookies.

But what if they had eaten all the cookies by now?

He remembered the way everyone had looked at him the night before. Daddy had seemed disappointed in him, and that had hurt a lot. Mommy had looked at him the way she always did, with a little smile that crinkled up her chocolate eyes and made him feel loved. Uncle Gabe and Aunt Lyss had just acted like they felt sorry for him.

He had gone to bed angry, angry with those children in the woods. This morning he was still . . . *gritty*. That was Mommy's word for upset, and that's how he felt. Gritty.

The children shouldn't have taken the cookies. It was stealing. And not only had they done something wrong, but what they had done had made Daddy angry with *him*.

"Sunny, stop!" To slow himself down, Jason grabbed at a low-hanging branch of the big old tree. This was where he'd been playing the day before, when he spotted the two children.

"Hey!" He peered into the woods beyond the clearing. But the trees were thick, and they went a long, long way — out across the field and up the side of the hill that overlooked the Farm. "Hey, are you in there?"

Sunny looked at him, then turned to stare into the trees. "Good dog," Jason whispered to her. "You can help me look."

Jason called out again, but all he heard

was the funny hacking sound made by a crow. A strong gust of wind whizzed through the trees.

Disappointed, he dug at the ground with the toe of his hiking boot. That's what Daddy did sometimes when he was trying to work out a problem in his mind. Maybe it would help.

He tried shouting into the trees again. No answer. But Jason waited some more. He didn't want to give up until he heard the sound of his daddy's voice, calling him back to the cabin.

Finally he turned to go. They should have come. They got him in trouble and then wouldn't come to help him. Maybe he didn't want to be friends with them after all.

That night, after Mommy had given him the last in a whole series of goodnight kisses and left his bedroom, Daddy stayed. He sat down on the bed and patted the blanket for Jason's hand. When he found it, he wrapped his big hand around it. Jason always felt good when Daddy held his hand. It made him feel safe, like nothing could ever hurt him.

"Jason, I owe you an apology," Daddy said. "About last night. I know you didn't take those cookies. I shouldn't have even felt the need to ask you if you did." He paused, then added, "If I hurt your feelings — and I'm afraid I did — I'm sorry, Son."

Jason looked up at Daddy. Even though his father couldn't see, he always seemed to be looking right at him when they talked. Like what they were discussing was really important.

"I just want you to know I'm sorry," Daddy went on, "and I believe you when you say you didn't take the cookies. Will you forgive me?"

Jason hadn't seen his daddy look sad very often. He almost always looked happy. Aunt Lyss said he usually looked like he was about to play a trick on someone.

But right now, he looked very sad, and Jason hated that. He sat up in bed and put his arms around his daddy's neck. "It's all right, Daddy. I forgive you."

"I guess we still have a mystery, though, don't we?"

Still hugging him, Jason nodded his head. "You mean, because we don't know who took the cookies?"

"Right. I know what you said, about the . . . children in the woods taking them. But —"

"You still don't believe they're real children, do you? You think I made them up."

"Jason, if they seem real to you —"

Jason pulled back. "Daddy, why don't you believe me?"

He saw his daddy take a deep breath, then run his hand over his chin. "Jason, I just don't understand how there could be two children out there in the woods. It's cold, and there's nowhere they could go to get warm. Who do you think these children are? And where did they come from?"

Jason felt a little better. At least Daddy was *trying* to believe him.

"Maybe they ran away from home."

"But they sound awfully little to be runaways, don't you think? And how would they get way out here?"

"I don't know," Jason said, watching his daddy's face. Daddy might be trying to believe, but Jason could tell he didn't. The apology made him feel better, but he wanted his daddy to *understand,* to believe him. The children were real. He hadn't made them up; he was getting too old for that kind of stuff. He guessed he would just have to figure out a way to prove he wasn't playing make-believe.

He hugged his daddy hard and kissed him on the side of his cheek, on that place where his black beard was thickest. He liked the way it tickled his nose. When he grew up, he was going to have a beard, too.

Long after Daddy had left the room, Jason was still awake. It was important for him not to fall asleep. He had to think, and he always found it easier to think when he was alone.

Tomorrow, when no one was around, he would talk to Uncle Gabe. If anyone could help him figure out a way to catch the children, Uncle Gabe could. He had once heard Daddy tell Mommy that Uncle Gabe was the smartest man he'd ever known, even if he did act like a clown most of the time.

If Uncle Gabe was that smart, he could help Jason prove he wasn't pretending. Or at least he would *try*. Uncle Gabe wasn't like most other grown-ups. He was never too busy to help. Never too busy to hear what a little kid like Jason had to say.

Next to Daddy, Uncle Gabe was Jason's favorite man in all the world.

SIX

Irritation welled up in Gabe as he stared at the empty container. Last night there had been enough baked ham not only for today's lunch but for topping two or three pizzas as well. Now it was gone. All of it.

"OK. This has gone far enough. It's no longer funny. I can survive on peanut-butter-and-jelly sandwiches the rest of the week if you can."

"What's wrong, Gabe?"

He scowled suspiciously at the group gathered around the table. Jennifer's puzzled frown looked sincere enough, but she had learned that deadpan expression of hers from a real pro. Nobody was more gifted in the art of the impassive stare than his old pal Dan.

Jennifer had been a quick study, all right. A few weeks ago, she had successfully convinced him that she'd had nothing to do with the fluorescent sign that had been placed in the middle of the town square. In shimmering neon colors, the sign had proclaimed the birthday of one *Gable Scott Den-*

ton, his age, and his telephone number — along with an open invitation for everyone to call, "after eleven tonight to give Good Old Gabe your regards."

After days of relentless digging, he had finally confirmed his suspicions. His wife and Jennifer had painted the sign, and Jennifer had erected it well after midnight the eve of his birthday. When confronted, Jennifer had given an incredible performance, first pretending to be horrified, then wounded that Gabe would point a finger at her. Not once did the woman actually lie to him; she simply skirted the issue. Only later, when she could no longer stand being left out, did she gleefully admit to her part in the escapade, confessing with what appeared to be a touch of pride that the entire caper had been her idea.

Small wonder that he wasn't the least convinced by the guileless stare she now leveled at him.

He sighed. "The ham, in case there happens to be one among you who is ignorant of the fact, is gone. At least," he said testily, "it's *almost* gone." He held up one small scrap of meat and dangled it between his thumb and forefinger. "Unless we want to divide this up for sandwiches."

"You're kidding." Lyss, his wife of mere

63

weeks, whom he loved to the point of derangement, ambled up beside him looking beautiful, curious, and convincingly vacant. He knew his lady well enough, however, not to be taken in by her charm. Love him she might, but she could be every bit as devious as her sister-in-law if she glimpsed the possibility of a good laugh at her husband's expense.

"How could it possibly be gone?" she asked innocently, peering down into the empty plastic container.

Dan was next. Gabe would have been disappointed, of course, if his friend's routine had not outclassed the combined efforts of all present. Dan lifted his Roman-gladiator chin and with casual disapproval remarked, "How could anyone lose a ham?" The inflection in his voice made it less a question than an accusation.

Jennifer folded her hands primly on the table in front of her and gazed at Gabe with a look of great wisdom. "Probably a 'coon. Or a wild dog. There are a lot of them around here, you know."

Jason was the only one who remained silent, and Gabe didn't have the heart to question the boy after all the fuss about the missing cookies the night before.

He sighed. Their fun and games were not

going to continue throughout the week. Not without a price.

He gave them his iciest smile and spoke with a tone usually reserved for a couple of rambunctious clowns in his church youth group. "All right, people. Enjoy your amusement. Just chuckle your way through the bread-and-butter sandwiches you're going to have for lunch . . . and dinner."

Lyss groaned, but he ignored her. "Sit," he ordered with an imperious nod at the harvest table.

Obediently, she shuffled across the room to join the others. They waited, all eyes riveted on him.

"Now, then," he continued, shifting easily to the role of maligned but forgiving patron, "let's look at the facts. We have a variety of items missing from the storage pantry — linens and assorted groceries. In addition, two dozen cookies and approximately five pounds of baked ham have disappeared within a twenty-four-hour period."

When no one offered to comment, he went on. "Since all present have vowed their innocence of any wrongdoing —" He paused, appraising each face looking up at him from the table. "The only conceivable answer is that somewhere on the grounds lurks an extremely clever, quiet, and well-fed thief."

A heavy silence descended upon the room. "You think it's one of us playing a joke. Don't you?" Jennifer asked.

Gabe fixed a bland expression on his face. "Why in the world," he drawled, "would I think a thing like that?"

They continued to argue good-naturedly among themselves for a few more minutes but got nowhere. Finally, with sighs of resignation, they put together bologna-and-cheese sandwiches for lunch. They ate quickly, without conversation. Jennifer and Lyss exchanged occasional wry glances. Dan, however, appeared to be giving the whole situation serious thought. He was uncommonly silent — so much so that Gabe began to wonder if he might have misjudged him. Certainly he didn't look like a man who was secretly enjoying a practical joke.

No one lost any time returning to their jobs at the campers' cabins after lunch. Only Jason remained behind, offering to help clean up.

"Well, cub, what do you think about our mystery?" Gabe asked, giving the boy's shoulder a squeeze as they put away the last of the dishes.

Jason studied Gabe's eyes for a moment.

"Do you think I made them up, too? The children in the woods?"

Gabe's smile faded. The small towheaded boy standing before him was obviously troubled. He wasn't sure how to respond, but Jason clearly expected something from him.

"*Did* you make them up?" he countered bluntly.

"No, sir, I *saw* them." Jason bit his lower lip.

Gabe studied him. "A boy and a girl, you say?"

Jason nodded solemnly.

"And you think they're responsible for our missing food?"

Again, the boy nodded, this time with a little more hope in his eyes.

Gabe began to stroke his mustache with his index finger. The kid was convinced. And while he didn't pretend to know much about little boys, he thought he *did* know Jason. And Jason didn't lie. One thing was certain: Jason really believed he had seen a boy and a girl in the woods. It was probably foolish even to consider the possibility, but Gabe had a hunch that it was important to Jason that *someone* believe him.

He narrowed one eye. "All right, cub. I think you and I might just try to catch ourselves a couple of poachers."

He dried his hands on the dish towel, then slung an arm around the boy, now bright-eyed with excitement. With a grin and a quick hug, Gabe propelled him into the great room.

"What we need," he announced gravely as they sat down on the slightly sagging couch, "is a plan."

They put their plan into effect shortly after midnight that night.

"I'm cold, Uncle Gabe," Jason complained, pushing closer to him.

Gabe tucked the boy's muffler more tightly around his neck. They were lying on their stomachs just below a rise at the foot of the field, not far from the huge old sycamore tree by the gate.

The night was cold, damp, and heavy with the threat of rain or snow. There was no wind, but the stillness felt like the proverbial calm before the storm. Gabe shifted uneasily.

Sneaking out of the cabin unnoticed had not been as difficult as he had feared it might be. Waiting until Lyss was deeply asleep, he had slipped quietly from bed, dressed hurriedly in the bathroom, then crept up the stairs to the loft. Instead of having to wake Jason, he had found the boy waiting for him, wide awake and impatient.

Now they huddled together in the brush. "You're sure this is where you saw them?" Gabe asked again. "This is where you talked to the little girl?"

Jason nodded, his eyes half-hidden beneath the blond, shaggy hair spilling out from his cap. "I tried to talk to the boy, too, but when he saw me, he grabbed the girl's hand and ran away."

Gabe studied Jason's face carefully. "What were they wearing, cub?"

Jason frowned and pressed his lips together. "The little girl had on a bright red coat," he said after a moment. "With a furry hood. The boy's coat was black, with shiny white pockets."

If Jason *was* creating all this from his imagination, Gabe thought, he certainly wasn't sparing any of the details. In spite of his earlier doubts, he was beginning to get caught up in his nephew's story.

"You said the boy looked to be about your age?"

Jason nodded eagerly. "But he's —" He searched for the word he wanted. "*Thin.* He's thin, Uncle Gabe. And he has dark hair, almost black, not light like —"

Gabe stopped him in midsentence, touching a warning finger to his lips and motioning to the far corner of the field.

Only yards away from where they were lying, a shadow moved from behind the end cabin in the boys' section.

Jason stirred, and Gabe quickly shook his head and put a restraining hand on his shoulder. As they watched, the shadow changed and broadened, then suddenly grew still.

It was difficult to make out anything other than dark, shadowy forms. Only one security light was on at this end of the field, and it was at the girls' side of the cabins. Gabe raised his head another inch or so above the rise, and Jason cautiously imitated him. When there was no sign of movement, Gabe began to wonder if they had seen nothing more than a clump of shrubbery being ruffled by the wind.

Then something moved. Gabe's eyes widened with disbelief as two small figures slowly emerged from the shadows. Jason caught a sharp breath, and Gabe warned him with a quick hug to stay quiet.

Even in the darkness, he knew what he was seeing. *Kids. Two kids. So Jason hadn't made them up after all.*

He held his breath, watching them. They hovered close to the cabins for a moment, as if to make sure no one else was around.

Suddenly, they took off, one pulling the other by the hand, in a frenzied run across the field. They were headed in the direction of the main cabin.

"That's *them*, Uncle Gabe!" Jason's whisper, harsh and excited, broke the silence.

Gabe gripped the boy's arm. "Shh! Stay down. Give them another minute, then we'll —"

"Look!"

Gabe swiveled around to look back at the cabins. Another shadow was emerging, this one much larger. The figure, crouching low but moving with agile grace, broke out of the shadows between the two cabins at the end and bolted across the field after the children. As he ran, he snapped his head back and forth, as if to make sure he wasn't being watched.

They were too far away to get a good look at his face, but Gabe could tell two things by the way he moved — he was a seasoned runner, and he was a grown man, not a kid.

A needle of fear pierced the back of his neck. Finding out that Jason's "friends" really existed had been a surprise, but not a frightening one. However, the realization that someone was with them — an adult — was far more unsettling.

Who were these kids, anyway? And who

was the man with them? What possible reason could they have for hiding at an isolated youth camp in weather like this?

"We're going to follow them," he whispered. "But don't let them see you." He pulled himself to his knees, helping Jason to his feet as he stood. "Until I find out what they're up to, we're going to keep our distance. Understand, cub?"

Jason nodded but tugged on Gabe's hand. "Hurry, Uncle Gabe," he whispered insistently. "We have to catch them!"

Gabe wondered uneasily just what, exactly, he intended to do when they actually confronted the two kids and their unknown cohort. This entire scheme might not turn out to be one of his better ideas. Here he was, out in the woods with a nine-year-old boy, chasing after three strangers who could be up to just about anything. The only other adult male he could count on was most likely sound asleep — not to mention the fact that he was also blind.

For one of the few times in his life, Gabe faced a situation in which he could not find so much as a trace of humor. All he could think of was the fact that the three most important people in his life were sleeping innocently and helplessly inside the main cabin while some creep and his two little sidekicks prowled around outside. And as if that weren't enough, the eager boy at his side — who had also become extremely important to him — seemed to have no idea that they might be in danger.

Staying low and out of sight, they reached the main cabin only a moment behind the others. A few feet away, a fruit cellar was banked against a small rise. Gabe ran around to the side of it, motioning for Jason to follow him.

A nearby security light cast enough of a glow on the end of the cabin that Gabe could see the furtive trio now standing on the deck, just outside the kitchen door.

He pressed against the side of the building to avoid being seen. With growing anger, he watched as the man on the deck, after a quick look around, took something from his pocket and inserted it into the space between the door and its frame.

At that instant Gabe realized that he was watching a burglar open the kitchen door with a plastic credit card. To his astonishment, the man stayed on the deck while the two kids went inside.

Furious, Gabe studied the man who now skulked across the deck, surveying one end of the cabin, then the other.

Now Gabe could see him clearly enough

to tell he was young — in his twenties, maybe — and appeared wiry and trim in a dark jacket and jeans. He was bareheaded, and his hair looked thick and curly.

An impatient tug on his hand reminded Gabe that Jason couldn't see around him. He frowned at the boy, then shook his head to warn him to stay put. Glancing from Jason to the cabin, his mind reeled when he saw the man ease himself carefully through the door.

"Come on," Gabe whispered to Jason. "We're going around to the window."

"What are we going to do, Uncle Gabe?" Jason whispered back.

Gabe shook his head, trying to ignore the knot of dread lodged in his throat. He reminded himself that, if these three were indeed their thieves, the worst they had done so far was to steal some food and supplies. If that were the case, they surely weren't all that dangerous.

Besides, even if they did decide to make trouble, he thought he could handle two kids and a man who looked to be several inches shorter and twenty pounds lighter than himself.

They climbed the steps and tiptoed across the wooden deck as quietly as possible. Gabe moved Jason safely behind him, then edged closer to the window.

He tried to be quiet, but he found it almost impossible to move without making a racket. His feet felt like frozen clubs in the sturdy hiking boots, and his legs were stiff and unsteady from the cold air and tension. Carefully he plastered himself against the wall of the cabin and looked through the side of the window.

At first, he could see nothing. There was no light inside the room, and the faint glow shed by the outside security light was only enough to cast shadows.

Then one of the shadows moved, arcing a thin stream of light from corner to corner across the room.

Gabe stiffened. A flashlight! No doubt so they could see what they wanted to steal.

He pressed the side of his face even closer to the glass. The shadows revealed only one of the children — the boy — who was now moving toward the storage pantry.

Gabe inched closer, trying to see the far end of the kitchen. He stifled a small murmur of disappointment when he saw that the man was standing right beside the door.

His eyes scanned the room, and he moved in closer for a better look. There was the little girl, bathed in a soft wash of light from the open refrigerator door. Apparently, she was about to help herself to the contents.

Gabe pressed his lips together in a tight, angry line. At his side, he felt Jason squirm. He glanced down at him, again warning him with a finger over his lips to remain quiet.

A soft thud from inside made him turn back to the window. The refrigerator door was shut and the flashlight had been doused.

All movement inside the room had ceased. With a pounding heart, Gabe's eyes locked on the dark form now standing in the doorway between the kitchen and the great room. Even in the darkness, he immediately recognized the towering silhouette.

Dan! What did he think he was doing, walking right into the midst of those three, when he couldn't even see what was going on. . . .

Gabe stared through the glass. Dan might not even know anyone was *in* the kitchen. Had he heard something and come to check — or had he simply walked into the room and stumbled onto them unknowingly?

Either way, his being there meant there was no more time to waste.

Gabe looked desperately around the deck, hoping to find some kind of weapon. But there was nothing, only a few empty clay pots and a discarded milk can.

Jason huddled against him, shivering. *What should he do now?* The guy inside might have a gun . . . or a knife . . . and there was Dan, who couldn't even see the others in the room. The women were probably still asleep.

Whatever he did, it had to be quick.

His decision made, Gabe gave Jason a quick, urgent directive, then began moving toward the kitchen door.

SEVEN

Daniel immediately identified the sound he had heard upon entering the kitchen. Someone had just closed the refrigerator door.

So Gabe wasn't sleeping either. Good. He was wide awake and hungry himself. Might as well have some company.

"Gabe?"

He waited, confused by the silence.

"Lyss?"

Not a chance. Lyss wouldn't waste her sleep time on anything, even food.

Then it dawned on him. "Jason. Don't try to sneak past me." He walked on into the room. "You'd just better hope there's plenty of that pudding left, sport." He stretched out a hand, waiting for Jason to take it.

Only after a moment of absolute silence did Daniel begin to sense something wrong. Jason would have come to him, would have at least said something. Nor was it Gabe or Lyss. The two of them were great pranksters, but they never took advantage of his blindness. And he had left

Jennifer still in bed, sound asleep.

Still another few seconds passed before a warning buzz finally went off in his mind.

There was someone in the kitchen, all right . . . but who?

He seldom used Sunny on harness in the cabin; the surroundings were comfortably familiar, and he didn't need her guidance to get around. Now, however, he wished he had brought her into the kitchen with him.

Daniel's heart skidded to a stop, then raced. He stood unmoving, suddenly frightened.

Were the lights on? If so, he was an open target for whoever might be watching. He lifted his chin and forced his voice into an authority he didn't feel. "Who's there?"

He waited, his chest tightening. "I said who's there?"

Silence was his only reply. Yet he was absolutely certain he wasn't alone.

For the first time in months, a familiar attack of vertigo hit him — a dizzying assault that bordered on panic, the kind that had so often seized him during those first few months after the automobile accident. He felt himself watched by an unknown adversary. He was exposed. Vulnerable.

Perspiration bathed his face, and he reached out for something to steady himself.

With relief, he felt the edge of the large, vintage cabinet, clung to it, and waited.

Teddy stood frozen in place only inches from the door. He squinted into the shadows, trying to get a good look at the dark giant now standing in the middle of the room.

Silhouetted in the glow from the outside light, the guy looked huge, with shoulders broad enough to block Teddy's view, and arms that, even in a bathrobe, spelled muscle.

He glanced at Stacey. In the dim light from outside, he could see that the poor little kid looked like someone had shot an electric current through her system. Her dark eyes were round and frightened, her mouth half-open in astonishment.

Nicky, ducking his head out of the storage pantry at the sound of a strange voice, reached his little sister's side in three broad steps and hunched himself protectively between her and the big guy in the bathrobe.

For the second time, the giant spoke. "I said who's there?"

Obviously, he couldn't see too well in the dark. Teddy fleetingly wondered why he hadn't turned on the lights. One thing was certain — they had only seconds if they were going to get out.

With one hand, he threw the door open; then he jumped aside, yelling, *"Run! Now!"*

The words were no more than out of his mouth when a blond guy in a blue ski jacket hurtled through the open door, blocking the kids' flight with his body.

Stacey, unable to avoid crashing into the man at the door, hit him hard enough to make her bounce and reel backward. She started to cry.

With a strangled exclamation of fury, Nicky charged the man and swung at him with both fists. But the man easily grabbed the boy with one hand and pushed him firmly against the wall.

Flipping the light switch with his other hand, he called out, "Dan — are you all right?"

Teddy took a step toward the door, and the guy in the ski jacket shot a warning. *"Freeze,* man! Don't even blink!"

Teddy looked at him. He didn't see a weapon, but something in that level, green-eyed stare stopped him.

"Gabe?" The big man in the white bath-robe looked relieved. Relieved and bewildered. "What's going on? Who's in here?"

Without taking his eyes off Teddy, the one called Gabe snapped, "Fagin and friends. But instead of picking pockets, they're looting the kitchen."

The dark-haired man looked even more puzzled. "What?" His frown deepened as he turned in Stacey's direction. "Who's crying?"

Teddy studied the bearded man with dawning understanding. *The guy was blind!*

They could have gotten away! If it hadn't been for that hard-eyed linebacker, they could have gotten away without anyone being the wiser. He made a choked sound of disgust, and the guy in the ski jacket shot him a withering look.

Suddenly the room exploded with noise as a big golden retriever came charging into their midst, snarling and barking like a wild thing.

Teddy's stomach lurched when he saw the dog zero in on him, roaring its intention to attack. Instinctively, he flung his arm across his throat.

Stacey, still crying hard, screamed in terror.

The blind man stopped the dog with a sharp command. The retriever dug in with all four paws, lowered its head, and silently continued to challenge Teddy with a menacing glare.

"Stacey," Teddy was dismayed at the

weak sound of his own voice. "It's OK, baby. Be quiet now."

She looked at him, her dark eyes uncertain, her tear-tracked face pinched and frightened. Gradually, her sobs quieted, but she continued to watch Teddy with an uncertain gaze.

Just then a good-looking woman in a furry robe came racing through the door. She ran up to the blind man and grabbed his arm. "Daniel! What's wrong? I heard —"

She turned from him to scan the room, her mouth falling open in bewilderment as her gaze came to rest on Teddy, then the children.

Teddy's head swiveled when another woman came marching out of the room behind the kitchen. She was tall, with hair the same charcoal color as the blind man's. She was wearing a plaid bathrobe a couple of sizes too big for her, and she looked irritable and sleepy.

"Gabe, what is going on out here? Do you guys have any idea what time it —"

She stopped just past the doorway, staring blankly at the assembly in the kitchen, shaking her head as if to clear it.

The room was a din of confusion and noise. Everybody started talking at once. The dog began to bark again, and Stacey renewed her crying. Teddy's mind whirled.

The woman in the fuzzy green robe broke into the bedlam with a sharp voice. "Daniel, where is Jason?"

Teddy stared at her. *How many people were crammed into this place, anyway?*

The blond guy answered. "Outside. In the fruit cellar. I told him to stay there until I came after him."

"The *fruit cellar?*" the woman repeated, her dark eyes widening with disbelief. "Why in the world did you put Jason in the *fruit cellar?*"

"Later, Jennifer," the linebacker snapped. "Right now, let's find out what's going on with our . . . *guests* here. I'll fill you in on the details later. Don't worry. Jason's fine."

"Well, for goodness' sake, I'm not going to leave him out there in the cellar!" the woman said, her eyes flashing with anger. She started toward the door, but the blind man reached for her.

"Don't go out there, Jennifer —"

She shrugged out of his grasp and went on, stopping at the door to rake Teddy's face with a look of incredulous fury. "There can't be anything *outside* to worry about, Daniel. All the trouble seems to be in *here!*" She slammed the door hard on her way out.

It was quiet for a moment, as if most of

the excitement in the room had followed her outside. The only sound was Stacey's choked weeping.

The blond man named Gabe glanced at the little girl, then turned to Nicky. "Are you her brother?" he asked sharply.

The boy leveled a hostile stare at him and nodded, saying nothing.

"Then take care of her," he ordered curtly.

With interest, Teddy noticed that the linebacker's eyes, hard with anger only a few minutes before, softened as he watched Nicky go to his sobbing little sister and try to comfort her.

Nicky put his arm around Stacey, then coaxed her to sit down on the long bench behind the table. Pulling a handkerchief from his pocket, he pushed it at her, saying, "Stop crying now, Stacey. And blow your nose."

As if surprised to hear his voice, she quieted. She looked up at Nicky, then down at the crumpled handkerchief in his hand. After a second, she twisted up her mouth and said, very distinctly and with obvious distaste, "It's not clean. I don't want it."

Nicky scowled. "It's the only one I have. Use it."

Hearing the gruffness in his voice, she

puckered her mouth and began to cry all over again.

The blond man looked at her for a moment, then, keeping one eye on Teddy, moved to the large white cabinet beside the blind guy, opened the bottom door, and tore off a paper towel from its rack.

He walked over to Stacey, stooped down, and offered her the towel. "Here. This is clean."

The little girl raised her eyes to the linebacker. She studied him thoroughly for a few seconds, then reached out a small, mittened hand and took the towel, dabbing awkwardly at her nose. With her other hand, she pulled the hood of her coat down, away from her face, revealing her stubby pigtails.

She wiped her nose, staring at the man. "Please, I want Mrs. Whispers," she said in a shaky voice.

The man frowned. "Who?"

Stacey pointed across the room, where her rag doll lay on the floor in front of the refrigerator.

Awareness dawned in the blond man's expression, and he went over and picked up the doll. When he returned and handed it to her, Stacey immediately hugged the doll fiercely to her heart. "Thank you," she said with surprising dignity between sniffles.

The man studied her for a minute. "Why did you name her Mrs. Whispers?"

"It's a secret," she said gravely. "I can't tell you."

He stared at her, then nodded. "Right."

Teddy saw his expression sober as Gabe walked over and started talking in a hushed tone with the blind man — probably, Teddy thought, to brief him on the situation in the kitchen.

A stab of anger sliced through Teddy as he looked at the kids — anger at himself for being stupid enough to get caught like this. These people would call the police, of course. And that meant further delay in getting to Virginia. His jaw tightened as he realized how little protection the local police would be. There wasn't a community police force in the country that was any match for the Family's henchmen.

His gaze went to the door when it opened. The woman in the green robe walked in, holding the hand of a small boy in a heavy coat and a knitted cap. The thatch of blond hair Teddy could see escaping from the child's cap was almost white, but the boy had eyes as dark as his own. He looked to be about Nicky's age, but when he spoke, his speech sounded like that of a younger child. Of course, Nicky talked more like an adult than a nine-year-old, so Teddy couldn't be sure.

"That's them, Mommy! I told you! Didn't I tell you?!"

He pulled free of the woman and marched up to the other two children. "Why did you run away from me? And why did you break into the cabin? You were stealing from us!"

Nicky's eyes darkened with hostility. "We weren't *stealing!* We were just borrowing what we needed for a couple of days. We were going to pay you back."

"Jason —" The blind man reached out a hand. "Come here, Son."

The boy went to him, but he continued to look back over his shoulder at Nicky.

The blind man put his hand on the boy's shoulder. "Jason, are these the children you saw? The ones you tried to tell us about?"

"Yes, sir," the boy replied excitedly. He looked at Teddy. "I didn't see *him*, though. Just the children."

Teddy studied the blind man. The woman had called him Daniel. The name somehow fit the man, Teddy thought. Strong. Solid. Teddy sensed that, blind or not, the big man standing in the middle of the room was very much like his name.

Daniel suddenly turned in Teddy's direction, as if he knew exactly what Teddy was thinking. "Who are you?" he asked bluntly. "What are you doing here?"

Suddenly Teddy became uncomfortably aware that everyone in the room was staring at him. Even the blind man seemed to be looking right through him with his piercing blue eyes.

"I think you owe us an explanation," the blind man said quietly. "And I think you'd better make it quick."

Teddy pulled in a long, resigned breath. "My name is Teddy Giordano."

"And the children? Are they yours?"

When Teddy hesitated, the man called Gabe shot him a look through narrowed eyes. "They're not, are they? What are you doing with these kids?"

"They're not mine," Teddy admitted. "But I didn't take them against their will, if that's what you're thinking."

"You don't even want to know what I'm thinking." The blond man's face was hard and cold.

The two men stared at each other for a long moment, then Teddy looked away. His gaze went to Nicky and Stacey, who were watching him with frightened, but trusting expressions.

"We're in trouble," he finally replied. "Bad trouble."

"You sure are, buddy." Again it was the blond man who spoke. His voice was deadly calm, but Teddy could feel the heat of his anger as he turned and started toward the other room. "I'm going to call the sheriff, Dan."

"No!" Teddy instinctively jumped toward him, and the man whirled, his eyes glinting with an unmistakable challenge.

Teddy looked from him to the blind man. "Wait. Please don't call the police. It'll only make things worse for us."

"I just bet it will," the linebacker said, his tone dripping sarcasm.

"Look, I know we shouldn't be here. But it's not the way it looks —"

"Right," the other sneered. "You were just making a late-night delivery."

"Why don't you just *listen* to him, mister?" Nicky turned on the man called Gabe, his black eyes snapping with frustrated anger. "We're not thieves."

"My mistake, kid," Gabe said harshly. "Where I come from, people who steal are usually called thieves."

The boy's angular jaw tightened, and with one finger he pushed his glasses up a notch on the bridge of his nose. "We're just trying

90

to stay alive, mister!"

Ignoring him, the linebacker turned back to Teddy. "What are you doing with these kids, anyway?" he asked. "Where are their parents?"

Without warning, the little girl jumped up from the bench and ran across the room to Teddy. He bent down and scooped her up in his arms.

"It's all right, baby," he murmured against one pigtail. "It's going to be fine. Don't cry anymore, OK?"

"Gabe asked you a question," the blind man said quietly. He hadn't moved, and the dog, settled by its master's side, continued to watch Teddy with a hostile stare. "Where are the parents of these children?"

Again, it was Nicky who hurled an answer.

"They're *dead!* All right? What else do you want to know?"

A small muscle just below the faint scar at the blind man's left eye twitched as he turned his face in the direction of Nicky's voice. "Both of your parents are dead, son?"

"Yes," the boy hissed at him. "Both of them."

Teddy could feel the barely controlled fury emanating from Nicky.

"Nicky," he cautioned, "stay cool." He

glanced from one man to the other. "Look — I've got money. I'll pay you for what we've used. I admit we took some food. And blankets and pillows." He dug his wallet out of the back pocket of his jeans. "Here, take this," he said, peeling off a roll of bills without even counting them and shoving them at the blond man, who shook his head in refusal.

"You'll pay, all right, buddy. But not *your* way."

Teddy glared at him in frustration.

"Are you in trouble with the police?" the blind man — Daniel — asked abruptly.

Teddy turned to him and uttered a small, harsh laugh. "I *wish.*"

Daniel frowned. "Then who?"

After a long pause, Teddy said, "You don't want to know, mister. Believe me, it's better that you don't know."

"You said you're in bad trouble," Daniel stated quietly. "Isn't that what you told us?"

Teddy hesitated, then nodded, forgetting for an instant that the man couldn't see. "Yeah," he mumbled. "That's what I told you."

"Then you need help. You and the children."

Teddy looked at him. It suddenly hit him that the blind man reminded him of Nick.

There was the same unexpected blend of kindness and strength in the man's face, the same gentleness and humor, that had marked Nick Angelini. Missing, however, was the gruffness, the tough mask that years of fast living and crime had baked into Nick's features. Nick had once told Teddy his whole life had been like a big spider web — a web he had woven and in which he had trapped himself with his own youthful foolishness and greed.

It was crazy. This man was a stranger, but suddenly Teddy knew he could trust him.

"We can't help you unless you tell us the truth," Daniel pressed.

The blond man and the two women were staring at Teddy with open suspicion. Teddy knew he had to give them an answer. He felt a sharp sting of guilt at the jeopardy in which he was about to place them. Ignorance was the only real defense against the Family.

But guilt took second place to desperation. He *had* to get the kids to safety. And if there was the slightest chance that these people could help him, he had to take it. Nick's kids were at stake. He had promised Nick. He would do whatever it took to keep that promise.

"All right," he said, turning back to the man named Daniel. "Let's talk."

EIGHT

It was after three in the morning before they finally called it a night.

Long before then, Jennifer and Lyss had found sleeping bags in the storage pantry and settled all three children in the loft bedroom.

Now the adults sat in the silence of the great room, drained from hours of talking and occasional arguing. Once in a while, someone would take a sip of lukewarm coffee or glance uneasily at the others. Mostly, they looked at Teddy Giordano, studying him, appraising him, wondering about him.

Not for the first time since Teddy had begun to tell his story, Daniel shook his head in a bemused gesture. "You've been here for nearly four days."

Teddy nodded. "We spent most of Saturday night in a motel just outside Morgantown. When I spotted the limo on our tail Sunday morning, I just picked a road and started flying until I shook them. We ended up here late that same afternoon. I saw the sign on the main highway," he explained, "and took a chance. I knew I wouldn't lose them for long if I stayed on the main road."

"Where's your car?" Daniel asked.

"In the woods. I covered it up with some tree branches and stuff. It's Nick's car, not mine — a big silver limo, hard to miss. But I think I've got it out of sight."

Fatigue seemed to overwhelm him as he rubbed his hands down both sides of his face and uttered a weary sigh. Jennifer watched him, wondering how old Teddy Giordano was. Probably not as old as he looked, she thought. With several days' growth of beard and his dark eyes hollowed by shadows, he appeared unkempt, haggard, and exhausted. Looking at him, thinking about the incredible story he had just related, she found it difficult to stay angry with the man.

"I never intended to stay this long," he said, still resting his head in his hands. His words shot out in a fast, staccato barrage that strengthened Jennifer's original impression of a tense, anxious person beneath the somewhat arrogant facade.

He dropped his hands to his knees. "I thought we'd hole up for a day or so, just until I was sure it was safe to leave again. But before you got here Sunday night, I tried to call the number in Virginia — the number Nick gave me. I found out that the federal marshal I need to talk with is in Florida until the end of the week." He lifted his hands, palms up, and shrugged. "I didn't know what to do. I decided our best bet was to just dig in here and wait."

"Are you aware that the little girl is running a low-grade fever?" Lyss asked him shortly. "Has she been ill?"

Teddy frowned. "No. At least, she hasn't said anything. I found one of those small electric heaters in the pantry," he admitted. "I thought it would take care of that little cabin."

"You're resourceful, at least," Lyss said, her tone softening. "Stacey may just be tired. Some children run a fever when they're tired. But she ought to stay warm and get some rest."

Frustration lined Teddy's face even more deeply. He flushed, then turned back to Daniel. "Look, I *am* sorry . . . about everything. My intention was to leave plenty of money behind us to pay for whatever we used. I'm no thief."

Jennifer heard an edge in Daniel's voice when he answered, even though his tone was pleasant enough. "You've been in the end cabin all this time? What if one of us had just walked in on you? We've been working our way down the row of cabins since Monday, cleaning and getting them ready for spring campers."

"I always knew where you were," Teddy said without hesitation. "I had your routine down. I figured you weren't going to get to us much before Friday. Besides, all we had to do was go out the back door and we'd be in the woods. That's one reason I picked the cabin on the end." He paused. "When the kids told me about your little boy seeing them the other morning, though, I held my breath the rest of the day, wondering if you'd come looking for us."

"Unfortunately," Daniel replied, a look of regret crossing his face, "no one believed his story. At least, not at first." He lifted his chin, frowning as if something had just occurred to him. "Two nights ago, late, Jennifer and I both heard a child crying. Was that —"

"Stacey," Teddy finished for him. "We, ah, we were leaving the fruit cellar, and she forgot her doll. She went back to get it, and when she ran to catch up with us, she fell." He glanced down at the floor. "She got scared, started crying. . . . She was pretty upset."

"No *wonder* the poor kid is sick!" Gabe snapped, his tone knife-sharp with disgust. "You've had her running around after midnight every night in thirty-degree temperatures! What do you expect?"

Slowly, Teddy raised his eyes to Gabe, answering his outburst in a tone that was unmistakably defensive. "We had to eat. And there was always someone around in the daytime. What was I supposed to do?"

Instead of answering, Gabe merely glared at him, then uttered a soft sound of contempt.

"I think we can understand your actions," Daniel put in, as if he sensed a brewing confrontation between the two men. "And I don't see much point in belaboring whether you were right or wrong. It's done now. But I've got to tell you that I think it would be a mistake to take those children out of here too soon."

Jennifer bit her bottom lip, anticipating an explosion when Gabe rose from his chair. His eyes glinted with surprise and angry disbelief. "Dan!" he muttered. "You can't mean it! This guy is Mafia! Who knows what kind of danger he's put us in just by coming here?" Jennifer saw Gabe's eyes dart toward Lyss, his expression fiercely protective. Gabe was easygoing, but when the people he loved were threatened, his temper could blaze without warning.

"I know you're concerned, Gabe," Daniel

said quietly, obviously trying to calm his friend. "And so am I. But I'm also concerned about the safety of these children." "What's done is done. They're here now. And I don't think we have much choice but to help them."

Dan turned back to Teddy. "You don't know exactly when this federal marshal will be back," he said. "You don't even know but what these . . . people who were following you aren't still around somewhere." He frowned as he leaned forward on his chair. "How long do you think you can keep running with those children?"

Teddy raked a hand through his already tousled hair. "What else can I do?" he countered. "The kids are tired; they're scared. I need to get them settled somewhere. And I *have* to get to that marshal. Once I deliver the notebook, maybe Sabas will lose interest in the kids and me. They're only after us now because I have something they want."

Daniel shook his head. "I wouldn't be too sure of that. They know you can probably finger the mob for your boss's murder. They may even think the children know something."

The significance of his words hung between them. Teddy stared, his face pinched and pale. "All the more reason I have to get the kids to a safe place soon," he finally said, his voice less steady now.

Jennifer watched him clench his hands together and crack his knuckles, once, then again.

He looked at her. "Their mother died of cancer four years ago," he said tightly. "Now they've lost their father, too. They're hurting. They're afraid. I've got to get them settled somewhere. They need a home. They're just kids. . . ."

At that moment Jennifer decided she liked Teddy Giordano. True, he was probably self-indulgent and shallow. He was sporting a watch that must have cost hundreds of dollars and a diamond ring that flashed its four-digit price tag every time he lifted his hand. His boots were obviously Italian, his jeans designer, and his sweater imported cashmere.

She had already detected more than a hint of arrogance in his manner, and she suspected a touch of the con man as well — a clever one, most likely. In addition, he seemed defensive and high-strung. Still, she also sensed a quick mind, a bold but generous spirit, and a great deal of loyalty.

When he looked at those children — even when he talked about them — his defiant dark eyes softened to an expression that looked very much like love. Jennifer decided that anyone trying to harm the Angelini children would have to get past Teddy Giordano first.

Daniel's voice broke into her thoughts. "Why don't you get yourself a sleeping bag out of the storage pantry," he suggested to Teddy, "and sack out with the kids upstairs for a few hours? Tomorrow is Thursday. You can try your man in Virginia again first thing and maybe still get help before the weekend." He paused. "Frankly, I think what you need to do is wait right here until someone comes for you and the children. You might be placing all of your lives in danger by leaving here."

"And he'll undoubtedly be placing *ours* in danger if he stays." Gabe got up and crossed the room. He stopped directly in front of Teddy Giordano, staring at him with open resentment. His eyes never left Teddy's face, but his words were directed at Daniel.

"Are you really buying this, Dan? The guy's admitted to being part of the *mob!* He could have *kidnapped* those kids, for all we know." His usually smiling face was taut with outrage. "Who knows what we'll bring down on our heads if we let them stay here?"

Daniel gently released Jennifer's hand. He got up and walked over to the fireplace, where a low flame was still flickering. He stood, his back to the fire. "You think we should force them to leave, then? What about the children? You heard Lyss — the little girl has a fever."

Jennifer watched Gabe carefully. The tension between him and Teddy Giordano had been obvious from the beginning. She doubted if either of the two men recognized the reason for the resentment between them. Most likely, she thought with a touch of irony, it was a case of one con man bumping heads with another.

Gabe's cynical, somewhat abrasive nature had been tempered years ago, when he became a Christian. But that didn't mean he wouldn't recognize a coat he himself had worn when he saw it on another's back. He just might be reacting, she mused, because Teddy Giordano reminded him too much of himself.

"Gabe?" Daniel prompted quietly.

Gabe looked at Lyss, then Jennifer. "We can't just kick the kids out into the cold," he muttered grudgingly. "And if they stay, I suppose *he* stays."

"If you think I'm wrong, Gabe, say so. You and Lyss have as much at stake here as we do," Daniel cautioned.

Unexpectedly, Teddy broke the exchange by hauling himself up off his chair. "I'll settle it for you. He's right. If we stay, we jeopardize all of you." He flicked an apologetic look at Gabe. "There's no reason you should stick your necks out for us. We'll go," he stated, looking wearier than ever. "As soon as the kids get a couple more hours of sleep, I'll —"

Gabe didn't let him finish. "Don't be stupid! You owe those kids whatever protection you can give them." His gaze swept Teddy Giordano with contempt. "Dan's right, unfortunately. You'll have to stay."

The two men stared at each other without blinking until Teddy finally inclined his head in a reluctant gesture of agreement. "All right." He paused, then added, "Thanks. I owe you."

Jennifer understood Gabe's reaction, even though she doubted that Teddy Giordano could. Dear Gabe — so much in love with Lyss, his new wife, so wholly dedicated and loyal to Daniel, his best friend and brother-in-law. Gabe would give up his life for anyone in this room — including Teddy Giordano.

But as caring as he was, Gabe could also be hard and unyielding when the people he loved were threatened. Teddy couldn't possibly comprehend Gabe's kind of love, a combination of toughness and tenderness, gentleness and strength.

When Gabe asked his next question, Jennifer half expected Teddy Giordano to tell him it was none of his business.

"Exactly how involved were you with these goons, anyway?" His expression was suspicious and openly hostile. "This guy you worked for — was he some kind of . . . godfather or what?"

Teddy looked as if he was about to smile, then seemed to think better of it. "It's not quite like the movies. No, Nick had a lot of power, but he was no *padrone*. He was what you've probably heard called a *capo* — a boss, a chief."

"And I suppose you were one of the Indians?" Gabe's tone was edged with sarcasm.

Teddy shrugged. "I was his driver. I drove the limo for him, raced a couple of his cars, worked on them, that kind of stuff. And I helped out with the kids — took them to school, to the doctor, to the dentist." With a level look, he added, "If you're asking was I into the action . . . no. Never. Nick made a point of never letting me near the business."

"How long had you worked for him before his death?" Daniel asked.

Teddy thought for a moment. "Nine, ten years, I guess. Since I was about sixteen. I worked part-time in a garage he owned when I was still in school. When I graduated, he took me off the street, gave me a job with him at his house."

Daniel nodded thoughtfully. "So you were close."

Teddy glanced away, and Jennifer saw a look of great pain cross his face before he hardened his expression. "Nick Angelini was good to me," he said flatly, his tone making it clear that he would say no more.

The room was silent for a long time. Finally, Daniel moved away from the fireplace and walked over to Jennifer, holding his hand out to her. "I think we're all in agreement about what has to be done. But before we turn in, let's pray about this."

Jennifer took his hand and rose from the couch. She saw Teddy Giordano dart a startled and embarrassed look in their direction.

After a moment's hesitation, Gabe took Jennifer's other hand, then Lyss's. Daniel offered his hand to the stranger in their midst, waiting until Teddy, with obvious reluctance, joined them in their circle.

Although Jennifer kept her eyes closed the

entire time Daniel prayed for their "new friends," she was sure she could feel Teddy Giordano studying each of them. She wondered if the troubled young man with the haunted eyes had ever heard anyone pray before. She clasped Daniel's hand more tightly, grateful as always for her husband's strength and goodness, and for the blessing of the family into which she had married.

Daniel gave her hand a gentle squeeze, as if he knew exactly what she had been thinking . . . and praying.

NINE

The snow began shortly after dawn the next morning, falling from a sky that Jennifer described to Daniel as a sheet of lead-colored canvas. Moderate at first, by midmorning it had increased to the kind of treacherous, wind-driven snow familiar to natives of the mountains. It came down fast, heavy and threatening. And as it fell, the air grew bitter cold.

The children cheered, but the grown-ups knew the storm was no laughing matter. Jennifer paced the floor. Lyss clanged about in the kitchen, dropping silverware. Gabe seemed to talk a little faster each time he looked out the window.

Eventually, Daniel began to drum his fingers absently on everything he touched. He had seen plenty of these spring storms in the mountains of West Virginia, and they were nothing to be trifled with.

During breakfast, Jennifer coaxed Gabe and Lyss into helping her clean the last two cabins on the boys' row. Daniel and Teddy agreed to stay with the children, who were begging to go out and play.

By eleven o'clock, Teddy had tried his call to Virginia three times.

Daniel heard him sigh with frustration when he returned to the great room after his last attempt.

"Still no answer?"

"No. I must have let it ring twenty times." He paused. "I don't know what to do."

Daniel was on his knees in front of the fireplace, trying to fix the stretcher on an immense old rocking chair beside the hearth. It had been his grandfather's favorite chair, then his father's, until Lucas had finally surrendered to his wife's plea to "retire" it. When he did, Daniel had immediately claimed it for his own.

"Not much else to do but wait," he said, half turning toward Teddy's voice. "Give me a hand here, will you? Just hold this steady for a minute."

Teddy braced the chair as Daniel forced the stretcher back into its opening.

"I can't believe it's snowing like this," Teddy muttered. "Isn't it supposed to be spring?"

Daniel smiled and cocked his head upward, his hands still working. "I grew up in these mountains, and believe me, this time of year anything can happen. The natives are used to unpredictable weather, but to outsiders it usually comes as a big surprise." He stood up, wiping his hands on his jeans and smiling at the sounds of laughter coming from outside. "Sunny's still in the yard with the kids, isn't she?"

Daniel heard Teddy move to the window. "She sure is," he said. "She just pushed Stacey into the snow, and now she's shoving at her with her nose. Stacey's obviously having a great time." He paused. "I think they're playing hide-and-seek. And I'd say your dog is winning."

"You don't beat Sunny at hide-and-seek," Daniel replied with a grin. "That's her favorite game." He walked over to the large pine table beside the couch and picked up his coffee cup, grimacing when he found it empty. "Lyss said Stacey's temperature was normal this morning."

"Yeah, she's fine," Teddy said warmly. "Are you two related, by any chance?"

"Lyss and I?" Daniel nodded. "She's my kid sister."

"I thought I saw a resemblance," Teddy said. "Is she a nurse or something?"

Daniel shook his head. "No, she's a teacher. Phys Ed." He started toward the kitchen. "Let's get some coffee. I think Gabe made a fresh pot before they left."

Teddy followed Daniel to the kitchen, watching as the blind man made his way to the stove. He lifted the coffeepot, and Teddy moved to help, then stopped. Obviously, the man knew what he was doing.

"There should be some clean mugs on the right-hand side of the cabinet," Daniel said, filling his own cup, then setting the old-fashioned porcelain coffeepot back on the stove.

After pouring his own coffee, Teddy joined Daniel at the table. He glanced outside to check on the kids, then stirred cream into his cup, studying the big man across from him as he did. For an instant, he sensed something familiar about Kaine. The feeling passed as quickly as it had come, but his curiosity remained.

Daniel Kaine had an unusual face — interesting, but not easy to read. Teddy supposed women would find him good-looking. Certainly, he had a kind of compelling presence about him. His bronzed skin made him seem robust, as if he spent a lot of time outdoors. His deep blue eyes were strangely unnerving as they followed the slightest sound or movement in a room.

Strong, Teddy concluded. This was a strong man. Even beneath his heavy black beard, Kaine's jaw looked firm, his chin stubborn. His dark brows were generous but not severe, and his prominent nose stopped just short of being hawklike. Teddy wondered about the small, vertical scar at Kaine's left eyebrow.

When Daniel lifted his arms above his head and stretched, Teddy had a sudden, peculiar sense of tightly harnessed power, a dynamic but fully controlled energy. Then the memory hit him.

"Daniel Kaine!"

Kaine lifted his dark brows in a question.

"I *knew* there was something familiar about you!" Teddy said excitedly. "I saw you on TV when you won the gold medal in the Olympics. You're the 'Swimming Machine' — isn't that what they called you?"

Daniel lowered his arms, a half smile crossing his face. "You remember that? You couldn't have been very old when I was at the Olympics."

"Oh, man! Do I remember? You were *great!*" Teddy exclaimed. "I was in junior high, but I'll never forget it." His words tumbled out with boyish enthusiasm. " 'Course, you didn't have your beard then, and you weren't . . ." He broke off, embarrassed.

111

Daniel, however, only smiled. "No, I grew the beard later. It's easier than shaving in the dark."

"Can you . . . I mean, do you still swim?" Teddy asked without thinking, then realized he might be out of line.

But Kaine didn't seem to mind. "You bet I do. Every day. I've got an indoor pool in my home," he explained easily. "That's why I'm feeling kind of stiff right now, going most of the week without any exercise."

"How long —" Teddy stopped. He didn't want to offend Daniel, but the question was burning in his mind.

"How long have I been blind?" Daniel finished for him mildly. "About six years now."

Teddy stared at him, feeling a sudden wave of sympathy wash over him. This man had been a national figure just a few years ago, an American hero. Now he was blind. Blind and doing odd jobs in a youth camp. Talk about lousy luck.

"So, you work here now, huh?"

Kaine started to take a sip of coffee, stopped, then smiled. "Well . . . just this week, actually. The couple who manage the Farm haven't had a vacation in a long time, so we came up to give them a break. As a matter of fact, we've been trying to find another full-time assistant for Mac — he's the manager of the camp. But until we hire someone, we're going to be helping out as much as we can."

"What is this place, anyway?"

Kaine briefly explained the idea behind Helping Hand.

"Then this is your place? I mean, you own it?"

"Not really," Daniel corrected him. "It's been in my family for years, but now it's owned by several people. When my Uncle Jake decided to retire, a group of people from my church agreed to help finance a camp if Gabe and I would get it going."

"So it's strictly for disabled kids?"

Kaine nodded. "Some of them stay here several weeks out of the summer; others just come for a week or two. It's been so successful that we've almost outgrown our facilities. We're trying to buy more land so we can expand, and, as I told you, we're going to add to the staff."

Teddy was intrigued with the idea. "But you don't actually live here?"

"No, we live in Shepherd Valley — that's about sixty miles from here. I run a Christian radio station there."

"A *Christian* radio station?" Teddy repeated, frowning.

"It's a radio station with a Christian pro-gramming format," Daniel explained. "The music we play — our talk shows — all of our programming is Christ-centered."

"I see," Teddy mumbled. He didn't, but he wasn't interested in learning more. That prayer circle last night had been enough for him. These people were church people, and church people had always made him un-comfortable. Daniel Kaine seemed to be OK — he didn't act like some kind of fa-natic. Still, he was obviously serious about his religion. *Too* serious, as far as Teddy could tell.

"Is there money in that kind of radio?" he asked abruptly.

Daniel laughed. "Not much, I'm afraid. But we make a living. I do some counseling part-time, too. We get by."

They both smiled when they heard Stacey squeal with excitement, followed by the boys' laughter.

"I was really fortunate, having the station to go back to after the accident," Daniel said, continuing their conversation. "At least I didn't have to train for a new job. A lot of blind people have to take on a whole new career, and believe me, that's rough." He paused, then went on. "Learning to live without your sight is enough of a challenge.

If you have to learn a new job, too, you've got double trouble."

Teddy was quiet for a long time, thinking. "Yeah, I'm sure that's true. But I'll tell you, Daniel, there are times when the idea of a whole new beginning sounds pretty good to me."

Teddy glanced out the window. He could see Stacey down on her knees with her arms around Sunny's neck, giggling as the retriever nuzzled her chin. The two boys seemed to be hitting it off great, too.

He turned back to Daniel Kaine. "Sometimes I wish . . ." He stopped, surprised at what he was feeling. "Sometimes I wish I could just . . . be a different person. Start all over, from scratch. A brand new life." He laughed at his own foolishness. "Crazy, I know."

Daniel shook his head. "Not so crazy. There are a lot of people who probably feel the same way. Sometimes it's the only thing to do."

Teddy uttered a small, humorless laugh. "And sometimes," he said bitterly, "it's the only thing you *can't* do. Your past is your past, man. And it's always with you."

"Unless you're willing to give it up," Daniel replied.

Teddy looked at him but said nothing.

They were silent for a long time, during which Teddy found himself thinking about his past, especially about his family.

Things hadn't been so bad before his dad died, he remembered. He and his older sister, Gina, had always had to work to help out at home, but their parents had been decent to them. But his dad had died when Teddy was only eleven, and a year later his mother remarried. Jack Falio had immediately judged his new stepson to be a "wise-mouthed kid," a "son with no respect." Teddy thought Falio was a hardnose, and an old-country jerk.

At the same time, Gina had married and left home. Feeling deserted by his sister and betrayed by his mother, Teddy had made no effort to get along with his stepfather. When a new little half sister came along, Teddy started drifting farther and farther away from his mother and the home that, by then, had come to seem like a prison.

For the next two or three years, he spent most of his time on the street with a small-time gang. Later he picked up pocket money by doing odd jobs at a garage owned by Nick Angelini. "Nicky Angel," the other *capos* called him.

Nick Angelini didn't spend much time around the garage, but he kept a close eye on his employees, even a part-time flunkie like Teddy. For some reason, the older man took a liking to the defiant teenager, eventually putting him to work full-time, even letting him race a couple of his cars professionally. Finally, he asked Teddy to move into his home and become his driver.

Teddy didn't have to be asked twice. In spite of the fact that Nick Angelini was a known boss for P. J. Sabas, Teddy was in awe of the big, good-natured Sicilian. If Nick had tried to bring him into the business, he wouldn't have hesitated.

Surprisingly, though, Nick had made it clear from the beginning that Teddy was to stay clean. He took him under his protection, much as he would have a son or a younger brother. The closest Teddy ever got to the action was overhearing an occasional phone conversation between Nick and one of the other *capos*.

Teddy knew what Nick's business was, and he knew it was dirty business. But he told himself it didn't matter. In his own way, Nick was a good guy. He was good to his kids, good to Teddy, good to his friends. So he was mixed up with the mob. So what?

Daniel's voice startled him out of his thoughts. "What would you do, Teddy, if you could start over again? What kind of life would you choose for yourself?"

Teddy looked at him. He was surprised at how easily he could answer Daniel's question. He had never really thought it all out. But over the years, he had daydreamed about the way he'd like to live . . . if things had been different.

"I'd get out of the city, for starters," he said. "I grew up on the streets, and I hated it. The noise, the stench, the traffic. One reason I liked it at Nick's so much was that we lived outside town. It wasn't like this, you understand, on a farm and all; but at least the air was cleaner, and it was quiet most of the time." He hesitated. "I even had a garden."

"A garden?" Kaine smiled a little.

"Yeah. A *good* one, too. The kids helped me. We had flowers on one end and vegetables on the other. It was a beauty."

"So you like being outside. What else? If you could start over again, I mean?"

Teddy smiled to himself. "It's pretty wild, I guess."

"Some of my daydreams are, too." Daniel Kaine leaned back, crossing his arms comfortably over his chest, waiting.

"Well . . . I know it's impossible —" Teddy stopped, then went on. "But if there were any way I could, I'd . . . adopt the kids. Nicky and Stacey." He waited, expecting Kaine to laugh. Or maybe even frown in disapproval.

Daniel Kaine did neither. Instead, he dropped his arms and leaned forward, resting his hands on the table in front of him. "That doesn't really surprise me, Teddy. I hear your love for those children in your voice every time you talk to them. Or about them."

Teddy swallowed hard. "Yeah . . . well, we both know it's never going to happen. But you're right. I really do care about the kids. They're like my own, you know? And I think they care about *me*, too."

"Yes," Daniel answered softly. "I believe they do." After a moment, he said, "You know, Teddy — there *is* a way you can start over again. You might not have everything you want, just the way you want it. But if you really decide you want a fresh beginning, there is a way to do it."

Suddenly, Teddy knew what was coming, and he tried to head it off. "I suppose you're talking about religion?"

Daniel leaned back in his chair, a small frown creasing his forehead. Finally, he nodded. "Well — in a way. I'm talking about Christianity."

"I've already heard that stuff," Teddy

119

countered quickly. "I know the whole story, man. By heart."

A look of surprise crossed Kaine's face. "You do?"

"Yeah. Nora — that's Nick's housekeeper — she was all the time preaching at me. And the kids. She took them to church every Sunday, and she did her best to get me there, too."

"But you weren't interested." Daniel was still smiling.

"Not me. Oh, I went to church when I was a kid. I know about Jesus and all that."

"But you don't believe it?"

Teddy looked at him. "No, I don't believe it. At least not all of it."

"What part of it don't you believe?"

Teddy dragged in a deep breath. He liked this man and, without knowing why, wanted Daniel Kaine to like *him*. "Look, Daniel, where I come from, men don't *die* for each other. They *kill* each other."

His words fell heavily across the silence between them with the dull thud of reality.

Finally, Daniel nodded. "I see your point."

Teddy hadn't expected that. "It's just not for me, that's all," he muttered.

"That's where you're wrong, Teddy," Daniel said quietly. "It *was* for you."

Teddy stared at him.

Daniel sighed. "I think I know where you're coming from, Teddy. If you felt that your life was everything it should be, you wouldn't feel the slightest need to change it. Right?"

Teddy nodded, then caught himself and mumbled, "I guess so."

"But because you know your life *isn't* what it should be, you don't think you can have any part in Jesus, or that he wants anything to do with you."

Again, Teddy grunted his assent.

"You just can't quite swallow the story that one man would climb up on a cross and die for another man." Kaine paused. "Especially for a man like yourself."

Teddy looked at him but said nothing.

"Keep in mind, Teddy, that Jesus wasn't just another man. He was God . . . God in the flesh. When he did what he did, he was showing us a different kind of love . . . *his* kind of love. And the kind he wants us to have for one another."

Something about Daniel Kaine's assurance got to Teddy. Suddenly, Kaine was making him angry. "Nobody — *nobody* — willingly puts their life on the line for someone else! If you believe that, man, you've been out of the real world too long! Maybe, just maybe . . . if Jesus *was* God, like you say, he would do it. But *if* he did it, it wasn't for people like me."

" 'Very rarely will anyone die for a righteous man, though for a good man someone might possibly dare to die.' "

"That's what I'm saying. . . ."

" 'But God demonstrates his own love for us in this: While we were still sinners, Christ died for us,' " Kaine finished softly.

Teddy blinked, saying nothing as he realized that Daniel Kaine had been quoting from the Bible.

"Those are God's words, Teddy . . . not mine."

Teddy started to interrupt, but Daniel stopped him with a quick gesture. "Wait. Bear with me. This is for you, Teddy. 'It is not the healthy who need a doctor, but the sick. I have not come to call the righteous, but sinners to repentance.' Wait —," Daniel said again, almost as if he could see Teddy's attempt to protest. "There's more. 'He died for all. . . .' *All* Teddy. No exceptions. Just one more verse, OK? 'Therefore, if anyone is in Christ, he is a new creation; the old has gone, the new has come!' "

Kaine grinned. "Now, isn't that exactly what you're talking about?" He didn't give Teddy the opportunity to answer but went on in the same casual, good-natured tone. "It surely sounds to me," he said, "as if God wrote the answer before you ever asked the question."

Abruptly, Kaine stood up. "I'm going to lend you Jennifer's Bible — mine's in Braille," he said with a smile. "Maybe you might pass a little time today by reading through the Gospel of John." He started to leave the table, then turned back. "If you're a fast reader and want to find out more about this subject of new beginnings, go on to Romans."

"The Bible's hard for me to understand," Teddy said grudgingly.

Daniel grinned at him. "You ought to try reading it in Braille sometime, friend," he said dryly. Counting off his steps, he walked out of the room.

TEN

By early evening, the tension in the cabin had sharpened until it was almost palpable, especially between Gabe and Teddy Giordano.

Jennifer knew Daniel was also feeling the strain. Earlier he had confided to her that he was particularly bothered by the fact that the snow had begun just after dawn. Both his grandfather and his Uncle Jake were men who knew these West Virginia mountains as well as they knew the inside of their own homes, and they always insisted that the worst snowstorms were those that began shortly after the first light of day. Their observations weren't infallible, but Daniel had seen enough mountain winters in his own time to be wary of the storm now in progress.

Under ordinary circumstances, being snowed in with her husband and family wouldn't have bothered Jennifer in the least — it would have been fun. Present circumstances, however, were anything but ordinary. Even the normally imperturbable Lyss had a flinty edge in her voice. Only the children seemed reasonably untroubled by their situation, although she had caught Nicky staring apprehensively out the window a couple of times.

Hour by hour, the day had trudged by into evening, clouded by a peculiar overtone of unreality. They did their work, ate their meals, made the obligatory small talk, and avoided discussion of the snow that continued to fall in a steady white onslaught.

At seven forty-five, Teddy again tried to reach someone with the Federal Witness Protection Program. Jennifer was surprised but relieved when she heard him begin a conversation. When he returned to the others at the far end of the great room, however, his cheerfulness seemed halfhearted.

"At least I got an answer this time," he said with an uncertain smile.

"That's good," Daniel said. "What did you find out?"

"I still didn't talk with Nick's contact," Teddy replied. "But the man who answered *is* a federal marshal, and he seemed to think the marshal who arranged everything with Nick is back in town. He promised to have someone call me within the hour. He said if he can't connect with the other marshal, he'll make the arrangements himself to get us out of here."

"That should make you feel better," Jennifer said, trying to smile. She and the children were sitting at a small table in the corner, stalled in what seemed to be an endless game of Monopoly. Stacey was too young to comprehend the strategy, yet insisted on being a part of the game, and Jennifer was too restless to concentrate. Consequently, Nicky had easily captured the board.

The children were getting tired — tired and irritable. Jennifer could hear it in their voices. And Gabe wasn't much better. He was as restless as she had ever seen him. She sighed, then brightened a little when Daniel suddenly pushed himself up out of his rocking chair. "Let's make some music," he suggested. "It's too early to go to bed and too quiet in here to stay awake."

Ignoring the stony silence that greeted him, he pushed up his sweater sleeves and said firmly, "Come on now. We're not going to stop the snow by sitting around worrying about it. Lyss, have you finished that dulcimer for Jennifer yet?"

"Mm."

"If that was a yes, go get it. Gabe, where's your fiddle? Jason, will you find my guitar for me, please? And get your Aunt Lyss's banjo, too."

Jason suddenly came to life, hopping off his chair and running to the corner of the room where Daniel's guitar and Lyss's banjo were propped against the wall.

With the help of the three now wide-awake children, the adults also seemed to find a reserve of energy. While Gabe tuned his fiddle, Jennifer oohed and aahed over the new dulcimer her sister-in-law presented to her.

Gabe even managed a civil comment to Teddy Giordano. The younger man was openly admiring of the finely crafted, hourglass-shaped instrument. "You *made* that?" he asked Lyss. "What *is* it, some kind of guitar?"

"Same family, but older," Gabe said. "It's a dulcimer. Lyss custom makes them." His pride was evident.

Teddy looked from the dulcimer in Jennifer's lap to Lyss. "What's it sound like?"

"Show him, Jennifer. Jennifer plays a lot better than I do," Lyss explained. "I just like to make them."

Jennifer began to pluck the four-stringed, sweet-voiced instrument softly. "The dulcimer is thousands of years old," she said, continuing to play as she spoke. "It goes all the way back to ancient Persia. The immigrants who settled here in the mountains brought it with them from Europe."

"The thing about Lyss's dulcimers," Gabe said, "is that no two are alike. She gives every instrument she makes its own unique personality — its individual voice."

"Just like the Lord makes people." Daniel, tuning his guitar, turned slightly toward Teddy Giordano. "He made each one of us exactly the way he intended us to be." He stopped, his smile softening. "You know, it never fails to amaze me how God can take the discarded scraps of a life and shape them into something brand-new and beautiful."

Jennifer, by now accustomed to Daniel's analogies, glanced from her husband to Teddy Giordano, then back to Daniel. She sensed a definite current between the two men — nothing hostile, but a kind of *challenge*, perhaps.

Delighted with the dulcimer, she continued to pluck it lightly. "Lyss, it's beautiful! It's *exactly* what I wanted!"

"Sing, too, Mommy," Jason begged, plopping down on the hearth and motioning for Nicky and Stacey to join him. Teddy Giordano followed the children over to the fireplace, dropping down beside Stacey and settling her snugly against his side.

Jennifer began to play and sing "Wild-wood Flower," a sad old folk ballad about lost love. After a moment, Daniel added his guitar and started to hum, then sing along with her.

They sang another mountain love song before Lyss and Gabe joined in with their instruments. When they switched to church-camp choruses, the children began to sing with them. Eventually, they played a little bluegrass, then turned to hymns before ending with a number of folk songs.

When they finally stopped, Stacey tugged at Teddy's sleeve. "Teddy, could I have a fiddle? Like that one?" She pointed to the fiddle in Gabe's hand.

Jennifer smiled at the sleepy-eyed little girl. Her stubby black pigtails were sticking straight out from either side of her head, and her round face was flushed with heat from the fireplace.

"Maybe when you're older, baby," Teddy said, giving her a hug.

Stacey's face fell, but brightened when Gabe made a beckoning motion with his hand. "Come here, kiddo. You can play my fiddle."

Jennifer looked at him, wide-eyed, then glanced at Daniel, whose dark brows had also shot up with surprise. Gabe's fiddle was no ordinary instrument. It had been hand-crafted by a master in North Carolina for an absolutely ridiculous amount of money, and it was Gabe's pride and joy. No one other than Daniel or Lyss dared to touch it, and even they were scrutinized by its owner's eagle eye the entire time it was out of his possession.

Now he was inviting a six-year-old girl — a child he barely knew — to play it?

Stacey squealed and went sailing over to Gabe, beaming as he allowed her to rake the bow awkwardly over the strings of the fiddle. Jennifer was fairly certain that that high-pitched screech very nearly sliced Gabe's spinal cord in half, but she gave him credit for being a good sport.

She saw Daniel shake his head and grin. Lyss, too, was gaping at her husband as though she didn't believe what she was seeing.

"No, no — you don't *push* the bow, dumpling —"

Dumpling? Daniel choked, then coughed, and Jennifer almost strangled at the look of amazement on his face.

"You draw it gently over the strings," Gabe went on. "That's it. Good, that's great! Try it again. Gently, remember.

Good! You're doing fine!"

Jennifer rolled her eyes at Lyss, who continued to stare at her husband in astonishment.

"Wait, wait, careful now. You don't want a *harsh* tone, dumpling. You want a nice, even, *sweet* tone. Like this."

By now, the feeling of contentment in the room, the warmth from the fire, the children's laughter, Daniel's occasional dry comments and Lyss's good-humored replies, had all worked together to lull Jennifer into a comfortable, drowsy tranquillity. Suddenly, the mood was shattered by a loud, angry bark from Sunny. Stacey cried out as the room plunged into darkness.

Still clutching the dulcimer, Jennifer leaped up from the couch.

Daniel also got to his feet. "What's wrong?"

Jennifer reached for him. "The lights went out, Daniel!"

He squeezed her hand and drew her a little closer. "The snow must have put too much weight on the power lines."

The faint light from the fireplace enabled them to see just enough to move around. Sunny stirred restlessly beside Daniel, and Stacey began to whimper.

His voice gentle, Gabe attempted to

soothe her. "It's OK, dumpling. It's the snow, that's all. Don't be afraid." Pulling her onto his lap, he began to rock her.

Jennifer heard a thump, then a muffled exclamation as Jason pushed up between her and Daniel.

"I hit my knee!" he mumbled, taking hold of Jennifer's hand. "Are you all right, Mommy?"

Jennifer smiled at the protective note in the small voice and bent to plant a kiss on top of his head. "I'm just fine, honey. I'll take a look at your knee when we get some light. Don't be scared."

"I'm not scared," he replied. After a moment he looked up at Daniel. "This is kind of what it's like to be blind, isn't it, Daddy?"

"Yes, it is, Son. Although I imagine you can see at least a little with the light from the fire."

"I wouldn't like being blind, Daddy," Jason said gravely.

"Well, Jason, I don't like it very much either," Daniel admitted. "But I've learned to get around fairly well in the dark. So right now, I want you and Sunny to stay here with your mother for a few minutes. Aunt Lyss and I will get some oil lamps and candles from the storage pantry, OK?"

"The snow must be awfully heavy, to knock the power out," Lyss said as she moved with Daniel across the room.

"How deep do you think it is by now?" Daniel had neglected to count off his steps and stumbled against the side of the cabinet. He muttered in annoyance, then went on.

"Gabe said he thought we had at least eight inches, maybe more," Lyss told him. "But that was earlier."

"Is it still coming down?" Daniel stopped as they reached the door to the pantry.

He heard Lyss go to the window.

"Heavier than ever," she said, her voice strained as she came back to stand beside him.

"There should be a supply of candles in the pantry," Daniel said, trying to reassure her. "What about oil lamps? Do you know where they are?"

"There's one in each bedroom, I think. And some in the great room."

"We've got plenty of drinking water. And wood. Gabe and I brought in several loads yesterday."

"We're going to need it tonight." She paused. "Dan? I'm a little worried."

Daniel slipped an arm around her shoulder. "What's the matter, Pip?" He had given her the pet name when she was still a little girl but seldom used it these days. He had heard the edge of fear in her voice, however, and for a moment, she was no longer a grown woman, but his little sister again.

"Lyss? What is it?" he prompted when she didn't answer.

"I don't know." She suddenly sounded very young. "I have . . . a really bad feeling. Like something awful is going to happen."

Daniel's heart constricted. Lyss was probably the most unflappable person he knew. She was a rock. Lyss simply didn't have *nerves*.

"It's been a strange day," he offered weakly. "With our unexpected . . . visitors . . . and the storm. And now the power going off . . ."

He jumped when she clutched his arm. "Dan, I'm afraid!"

In the silence following her tense admission, a gust of wind rattled the windowpane. Daniel had the sudden sensation of an oppressive weight bearing down on him, and he shuddered against the feeling. For one terrible moment, Lyss's fear became his own. Her alarm swelled to a wave of dread that threatened to engulf him.

He clenched his jaw and shook his head,

drawing in a shaky breath of relief when he felt the apprehension finally ebb, then disappear.

"You know what's wrong with you, Pip?" He tried to laugh, but his voice sounded painfully shaky, even to him.

"What?" Her grasp on his arm tightened.

"You've got Grandma Lou's heebie-jeebies," Daniel told her. "You know, the creepers."

Lyss's small laugh sounded forced. "You think that's all it is?"

Daniel nodded and squeezed her hand. "That's what it sounds like to me."

"You're probably right. I've let my imagination run away with me." Her voice sounded a little stronger now, and Daniel drew in a breath of relief. "Let's find some candles," she told him. "I don't do so well in the dark."

"Relax," he said dryly. "You're with a pro, remember?"

The combination of high wind and heavy snow had resulted in zero visibility. Boone squinted nervously into the darkness as the windshield wipers pushed the snow first to one side, then the other, grinding with the effort.

The limousine's headlights projected a

nightmarish, distorted scene into the darkness.

"What're we gonna do, Wolf?" Boone's voice trembled badly, as did his hands on the steering wheel. "It's impossible to see anything out there!"

"Pull off the road," Wolf said grimly. "I want to look at the map."

Boone went another quarter of a mile before spying a small house with a driveway that looked recently plowed. He eased the limo to a crawl and slid sideways into the driveway, letting the engine idle while Wolf studied a road map.

After a moment, Wolf looked up, glanced out his window, then leaned forward to look out the driver's side.

"What do you suppose that is?" he muttered, staring at a sign only a few feet ahead of them on his side of the road: HELPING HAND FARM — 10 Miles.

The sign was barely visible because of the blowing snow. Boone peered through the windshield, frowned, then shrugged without answering.

"Let's find out," Wolf said. "Get back on the road. I'll help you watch for signs."

Boone looked over at him. "Wolf, if it ain't right on the highway, we'd better not try to stop," he said, his tone petulant. "If

136

we get off the main road tonight, we may never get back on."

Wolf returned his attention to the map for another minute. When he glanced up again, he shot Boone a look that clearly said, What are you waiting for?

Boone muttered something under his breath, then started to pull back onto the highway. The wheels spun, and he slanted an I-told-you-so glance at Wolf. Again he coaxed the car, and this time the powerful limo moved backward, lurching only once as it bumped onto the road.

"Relax, Boone," Wolf said, without looking at him. "And go slow — I don't want to miss this place. If the snow gets much worse, we may need somewhere to hole up for the night. Whatever this Farm is, let's not announce our arrival. We'll just drop in on them unexpectedly."

ELEVEN

While Jennifer and Lyss placed lighted candles and oil lamps around the great room, Daniel stoked the fire, adding more logs and punching it up to a roaring blaze.

"We'd better call the power company before things get any worse," he said to Gabe as he replaced the fire screen. "Maybe they can send someone out by morning if we get our names on the list."

Gabe secured a candle in its holder and set it on the table by the couch. "I'll call," he told Daniel. Crossing to the other end of the great room, he began to leaf through the telephone directory.

Jennifer settled all three children in front of the fireplace. Taking one of the oil lamps, she started toward the kitchen, stopping when she saw the look on Gabe's face.

"What's wrong?"

He scowled at the handset. "The phone's dead."

Jennifer glanced from Gabe to the phone. "Try again."

It was no use. He tapped the receiver a

few times, then shook his head glumly as he replaced the handset on the hook. "Nothing," he said, his voice gruff, his face clouded with uneasiness.

Daniel, too, looked grim as he came to join them. "I was afraid of that," he said, raking a hand down his face.

"Afraid of what?" Lyss asked from across the room.

Gabe hesitated before he answered. "The phone's out."

Jennifer's stomach tightened. The expression on Lyss's face told all, and if *Lyss* was worried, maybe their situation was graver than she had first thought.

"What are we going to do?" Lyss touched Gabe's arm, her eyes fixed on his face.

"We're all right, babe." He managed a tight smile. "Relax."

"Gabe's right," Daniel seconded. "We've got the fireplace, plenty of food and water — and we'll probably have power in a few hours."

"I don't think so, Dan."

Gabe's flat disagreement seemed to surprise Daniel. "Why not?"

"We're going to have well over a foot of snow by morning if it keeps up," Gabe explained tightly. "They can't get through to work on the lines in this storm."

"So we wait," Daniel said with a shrug.

Jennifer studied her husband's face, wondering if he really felt as calm as he sounded. She realized then that she was counting on Daniel to remain unruffled. Daniel and Lyss. The two were always so steady, so cool-headed, that when either showed the slightest sign of anxiety it seemed to affect everyone around them.

She looked at Gabe, but he was staring across the room at Teddy Giordano and the children. When his gaze finally met hers, his expression was troubled and thoughtful. He glanced at Daniel. "Dan, I'm going to take the Cherokee and go into town."

"What? Are you *crazy?* You said yourself the utilities people probably couldn't get through."

"The Cherokee will."

A look of protest crossed Daniel's face. "No," he said flatly. "You can't risk it."

"Gabe, Daniel's right," Jennifer put in. "You *can't* go out in this —"

She stopped when he turned to her. She had seen that expression in Gabe's eyes before. He was going.

Abruptly he turned, flicking his gaze to Teddy Giordano and the children, who were still sitting in front of the fireplace.

"Giordano," he said, giving a quick jerk of his head.

"The phone's out," Gabe told the other man as he approached. "That means you can't get your call."

Gabe's voice was as hard as his eyes as he went on. "I'm going to drive the Cherokee into town and let the utilities people know we're cut off out here. If you want, I'll call that federal marshal again and explain what's going on. Maybe he'll give me some idea when they're going to come for you and the kids." As an afterthought he added, "They'll need directions, too."

Teddy looked at him. "I'll go with you."

"No," Gabe replied quickly. "You stay here. In case Dan needs help."

As Jennifer watched, the two men locked gazes. Finally, Teddy Giordano relented.

"All right," he said, nodding.

"*I'm* going with you." Lyss's announcement was quiet but firm.

Gabe whirled around. His jaw tightly set, he frowned. "No, you're *not.*"

Lyss was nearly as tall as her husband, and she met his eyes with a level gaze. "I'm going with you, Gabe. And don't use that tone with me." She paused. "I couldn't count the times I've heard you say that nobody in their right mind would venture out

141

alone in a heavy snowstorm."

"She's right, Gabe," Daniel said quietly. He turned toward Lyss. "But *I'll* be the one to go with him, not you."

Lyss faced her brother, her blue eyes so much like his now flashing with irritation. Even at five-ten, Lyss still had to look up to Daniel. But her tone was steely with resolve. "Daniel, Gabe's my husband. I'm going with him."

Daniel started to say something, then stopped, inclining his head in a gesture of understanding. "It's for you and Gabe to decide."

"You can be every bit as hardheaded as your brother, do you know that?" Gabe challenged, exasperation lining his features.

"You so often tell me, love," Lyss said easily, turning to walk away, "it's a family trait. I'm going to change into warmer clothes. You'd better do the same."

Gabe watched her all the way out of the room before turning back to the others. "Give me that phone number," he told Teddy Giordano.

Teddy pulled his wallet from the back pocket of his jeans. "Here," he said, handing a yellow slip of paper to Gabe. "If someone answers, repeat this number before you say anything else. The man you'll talk with

142

is named Keith." He paused. "Tell him to try to get someone here as soon as possible."

Gabe gave him a faint, unpleasant smile. "Oh, don't worry. I have every intention of asking for express service."

Daniel touched Gabe on the shoulder. "Gabe? Are you sure you ought to do this?"

Gabe hesitated for only an instant. "The snow is only going to get worse, Dan. And the longer I wait, the harder it's going to be to get out of here."

"You don't think you'll have any trouble making it into town?"

"The Cherokee's a tank, you know that. The old girl will take us anywhere we want to go." Gabe attempted a laugh, but it fell flat. "Relax, man, you're makin' me nervous."

Daniel's smile was also forced. "All right. But be careful. And get back just as soon as you can."

"Right." Gabe darted a glance across the room at Stacey, who was half asleep in front of the fireplace, her head bobbing against her brother's shoulder. A ghost of a smile flickered, then died. "Take care of those kids. They've had enough trouble," he said to Teddy Giordano as he turned to leave the room.

Jennifer shuddered and clasped Daniel's arm. "Daniel, can't you stop them? They shouldn't go out in this storm!" She felt physically ill at the thought of Gabe and Lyss leaving the safety of the cabin.

Daniel took her hand as Teddy walked away. "I don't like it any better than you do," he said, his voice rough with emotion. "But I'm afraid Gabe's right. Someone needs to go for help. We don't know how much longer this storm's going to last." His tone gentled. "It's probably not a good idea for us to be isolated out here. Not with these children to look after."

Jennifer tightened her grip on his arm. "Daniel . . . you don't think there's any way those people who are looking for Teddy and the children . . . could know where they are, do you?"

He pulled her to him and smiled. "Don't you have enough to occupy that busy mind of yours?" After a moment, his expression sobered. "Nobody's going to be out in this unless they absolutely have to be. I don't think you need to worry about Teddy's 'friends' showing up."

Jennifer leaned against him. He was probably right. But when another gust of wind rushed against the side of the cabin, she shivered and drew even closer against him.

144

She wasn't certain which bothered her more — the idea of being trapped out here alone in the middle of a mountain storm or the fear that they might *not* be alone. Either way, they could be in serious trouble.

TWELVE

The world outside was a nightmare, an angry bawling gale of shrieking wind and icy snow that burned their eyes and stung their skin. By the time Gabe and Lyss made their way to the garage, they felt as if they had been outdoors for hours.

The Cherokee was cold, too. Gabe turned the ignition key once, twice. On the third try it caught. He waited impatiently for the engine to warm up.

They sat in silence, both trying to ignore the wind lashing the frame walls of the garage. Gabe switched on the heater, but when Lyss shivered at the sudden blast of cold air, he quickly cut the fan.

"You sure you want to do this? It's not too late to change your mind," he offered, glancing over at his wife.

"I'm going," she said quietly.

"Crazy lady," he murmured. "Come here." He reached out his hand to her.

A smile rose slowly in her eyes as she moved into his arms. He gathered her against him, saying nothing for a moment,

146

simply holding her.

"I was afraid you were angry with me," she whispered against his cheek.

"No, babe," he said softly, moving to touch her lips with his in the gentlest of kisses, his hands going to her face. "I love you, Lyss," he whispered. "I love you so much it makes me crazy sometimes."

Gabe felt her catch her breath as he held her gaze, blinking hard against the tears in his eyes. He had loved Lyss forever. At times his love seemed almost too big, too overwhelming to contain. It would spill over from his heart and explode from his soul into tears of almost unbearable happiness, embarrassing him.

He kissed her again. He wished he could somehow put all his love for her into that kiss, but he knew no one gesture could ever begin to convey the depth of his feeling for her.

Finally he released her, touched her cheek just once with the palm of his gloved hand, then slid back behind the steering wheel. He looked at her with a shaky smile. "We'll want to try that again later and see if we can get it right, Alyssa," he teased.

Lyss smiled at him. "Unless you want to take us both out with carbon monoxide," she said dryly, "you'd better get this vehicle out of the garage. And buckle up," she added, fastening her seat belt.

Gabe backed out of the garage and slowly began to plow the Cherokee down the narrow lane.

"So this is where you disappeared to after dinner," Lyss observed, pointing to the partially cleared road.

"I put the blade on the tractor and took a couple of swipes at it. Thought it might be a good idea to open a road to the gate, anyway."

They reached the foot of the hill, went through the double gate, and started up the unpaved road toward the highway.

It was almost impossible to see. Without the security lights that usually illuminated the road, the snowy night was a thick black-and-white curtain, distorted and forbidding.

The Cherokee, however, plugged confidently through the snow, and Gabe finally felt himself begin to breathe a little easier.

He was secretly glad Lyss had insisted on coming along; he was grateful for her company. He wasn't all that worried about getting into town. He and Dan had taken the Cherokee through some pretty severe weather. But he had never shared Dan's love for winter. Gabe was at home in the mountains and had a native's respect for them. But if he were to be completely truthful, he found these spring storms downright scary.

"It's even worse than I'd expected," Lyss said quietly beside him, breaking the silence.

"It's rough, that's for sure," he agreed. "But we're doing OK."

She nodded and tried to smile.

"What a week, huh?" He glanced at her quickly, then turned his gaze back to the road. They were nearing the exit to the highway now, and he was feeling more confident. The state route might be snow-covered — there would not have been any extensive plowing done yet — but it should at least be passable in a four-by-four.

"It's been different," Lyss said, not taking her eyes from the road. "What do you think of our unexpected visitors?"

Gabe uttered a small grunt of disgust. "I wish they had found another place to camp out."

"You haven't been very nice, Gable." The only time Lyss ever called him *Gable* was when she intended at least a mild reprimand.

"What, I'm supposed to cozy up to the *mafia?*"

"Teddy's not really mafia," she protested.

"I think he's probably a pretty good guy. And the kids are sweet."

He shrugged. "The little girl is. Her brother's a little too wise-mouthed for my taste."

"All the more reason the two of you should hit it off," she said drolly. "You were every bit as precocious as Nicky when you were a boy."

"How would you know? You were still in diapers when I was a boy."

"Mm. But I was advanced for my age."

He grinned at her. The Cherokee swerved, and he turned back to the road. He righted the wheels and pulled onto the state highway, shaking his head in disappointment when he saw the condition of the road.

"Remember how I used to follow you and Dan around when you were in high school?" Lyss asked.

"Yeah. You were a real pest." Gabe knew she was trying to take his mind off the treacherous road conditions.

"I bet you never thought then that you'd end up marrying me."

"Hardly. I considered strangling you a few times but never marrying you."

She grinned at him. "Was I really that bad?"

"You were a brat." He smiled as he re-membered the long-legged, skinny, rather plain teenager she had been.

For years, he had thought of Dan's sister as a kind of younger sister of his own, prob-ably because he spent more time at the Kaine house than he did at his own home. To him, Lyss had been just another kid, a fantastic basketball player, and an incredible nuisance.

The first time he had seen her as a *person*, rather than an annoying extension of his best friend, had been one sultry summer night shortly after he and Dan graduated from college. The three of them — Lyss, Dan, and he — had gone to a circus on the outskirts of town. An hour or so into the performance, he and Dan had gone to get popcorn. When they returned, one of the male trapeze artists was standing on the sidelines, openly flirting with Lyss, who was seated in the front row.

Gabe's first reaction had been disgust. Lyss was just a kid, after all, and the guy looked to be at least ten years older than she. He wasn't sure whether he was more put out with the performer or with Lyss, reasoning that she should have known bet-ter than to carry on like that with a stranger.

As they approached, Dan had muttered

something about his little sister growing up, and Gabe had looked at her more closely. Lyss was no more than sixteen at the time, and while she hadn't lost all her coltishness, Gabe saw with surprise that she was no longer a child — and no longer plain. He stopped walking but continued to watch the repartee between her and the trapeze artist. Lyss was coy and somewhat awkward; the guy was confident and smug.

Gabe had been totally unprepared for the stab of white-hot anger that suddenly jolted him into motion. He spilled half his popcorn as he charged forward and planted himself between Lyss and the trapeze artist. With a gruff comment about robbing the cradle, he issued a veiled but unmistakable threat. His action caught Lyss so off guard, she was speechless. Only after the circus performer let go with a stream of incomprehensible invective in a foreign language did Lyss regain her composure enough to berate Gabe for "treating her like an infant."

The Kaine eyes flashing, she had sat haughtily between him and her brother for the rest of the evening, leaving Gabe to fume silently to himself. To make matters worse, Dan had worn a knowing smirk all the way home.

That had been the beginning. Somehow,

he had managed to wait two more years — miserable years of watching her date a football hero, a swim-team captain, and a computer guru — before facing the fact that, ridiculous and impossible as the situation might be, he was in love with Dan's kid sister.

Her parents had made them wait until Lyss graduated from high school before they began to date. Even though Gabe had been like another member of the family since grade school, he *was* six years older than their only daughter, and his interest in Lyss had come as something of a surprise to the Kaines.

Even more surprising — to Gabe, as well as to the family — the relationship endured, surviving Lyss's four years at college and a year working in Colorado afterward.

Within six months of her return home, she was wearing an engagement ring — but only with the understanding that they would not be married until they had the down payment for their first home in the bank.

Gabe was to learn that Lyss was never in a hurry. He was fairly certain they had had the longest engagement of any couple in the history of the county — almost five years. But now, finally, she was his wife, and he loved her in ways he was sure he could never have loved another woman. Lyss had been so many things to him for so many years — a kid sister, a buddy, a sweetheart, a confidante, and now his wife. It seemed that they had always been together, had always been a part of each other's lives. And it was good. It was extremely good.

Impulsively, he reached for her hand and squeezed it. "You know what, babe? I think one of the reasons I love you so much is because you're such a good sport."

"That's heartwarming, darling, to think that you married me for my sportsmanship."

"Yeah. You're a great basketball player."

"And you're such a romantic." She grinned at him, then sobered. "Gabe . . . you *are* happy, aren't you?"

He looked at her. "Of course I'm happy. What brought that on?"

Her smile was gentle. "Good. I want that for you. It's what you deserve."

He quirked one eyebrow. "Because I'm such a great guy, right?"

Lyss studied him for a moment. Her tone was surprisingly fervent when she answered. "Yes. You *are* a great guy. You're a truly good man, Gabe Denton. It's too bad you don't let more people in on your secret."

Gabe frowned dramatically and pressed a

finger to his lips. "Shh. You'll blow my cover, Alyssa. You know I don't —"

His words died in his throat as he came out of a particularly sharp curve on the narrow highway.

Coming toward them from the other direction was a large, dark car. Gabe squinted against the headlights, trying to get a better look. The other vehicle appeared to be a limousine.

On *this* road?

Abruptly, he skidded off the highway, bumping onto the snow-covered berm and jerking the Cherokee to a stop just before they would have slid into an enormous drift.

"Gabe, what are you doing?"

"I'm turning around." Gabe cut the wheel and backed up, rocking the Cherokee forward as he eased back onto the highway.

"What's wrong? Why are you going back?"

"How many limousines are you likely to meet on this road?" he bit out, keeping his eyes straight ahead. "Even in broad daylight in good weather?"

Lyss glanced at him, then turned to look out the front window. "You think it's them? The people looking for Teddy and the kids?"

His face was grim. "You bet I do."

"Gabe, be careful. Maybe we should go into town for help."

"In this storm it's going to take us another forty minutes just to *get* to town and maybe another hour to get back to the Farm. Anything could happen in that time."

Underneath the snow, the road was slick with ice and extremely treacherous. But the Cherokee was having less trouble than the limousine ahead of them. Within a few minutes the back end of the Lincoln had become visible, and they saw it fishtail twice, swerving dangerously left of center before darting back into its own lane.

Gabe tightened his jaw and gripped the wheel in a death lock, staying just close enough to the limo to be sure he didn't lose them.

Lyss leaned as far forward as her seat belt would allow. "I can't tell how many people are in it, can you?"

"At least two," he said hoarsely. "Maybe more. It's hard to tell."

"You don't think they're headed for the Farm, do you?" she looked at him. "They couldn't possibly know that Teddy and the kids are —"

She stopped when Gabe started into a narrow, wicked turn. Almost at once, he cut his speed. His stomach clenched as the

Cherokee started to slide, but with relief he felt the tires grip and hug the road.

"We'll stay far enough behind them so they won't know they're being followed," he told Lyss as they came out of the turn. "But I want to keep them in view just to —"

He broke off as he saw the limousine ahead zigzag and swerve. An oncoming semi, terrifying in the darkness and in its own immensity, fishtailed, then roared toward the limo on the wrong side of the road.

Panic slammed against Gabe's chest. He gripped the wheel, his hands shaking as he watched the truck start to jackknife, allowing the limo enough room to veer into the opposite lane and skid off the road untouched.

He clung to the steering wheel in a death grip as the semi kept coming, bearing down on them in a blaze of headlights, distorted by the wind-driven snow. He tried to swerve left, but the tires spun out of control on the ice.

The wheel wrenched crazily in his hands. He heard Lyss scream in terror, followed by the blood-chilling sound of crunching metal.

Then everything went black.

THIRTEEN

In the driver's seat of the limo, Boone sat shaking. With a trembling hand he reached for the door. "I'll see if we can help," he said. "It looks bad."

Wolf looked at him. "You just keep right on going."

Boone swung around, staring at Wolf in disbelief. "We can't do that! Those people may be hurt bad! We've got to see if we can help!"

"I said we don't stop," Wolf replied with chilling indifference. "Now get out of here before another car comes along."

In the back, Arno fidgeted. He secretly agreed with Boone. They ought to stop. But he wasn't about to argue with Wolf.

"There might not be another car along for hours, Wolf," Boone again tried to protest. "Not in this storm."

"It's a state highway. That truck driver was on the road, wasn't he? There'll be other cars. Now *move!*"

Boone eyed him for another few seconds, his mouth quivering. Arno followed his gaze as he finally turned to stare out the window at the accident. The semi and the Cherokee were meshed together in a silent, terrible embrace. Finally, Boone pulled forward. The car slipped, then leveled off, and they went on.

A tomblike silence enveloped the interior of the limousine for a long time. At last Wolf turned, and as his eyes caught Boone's, he smiled. "Turn off up there, Boone — at that sign," he said mildly, again looking back to the road. "Let's find out what this *Helping Hand Farm* is."

Gabe struggled toward consciousness, fighting against the pain. It held him prisoner, the weight of it pressing down on his head, his shoulders, suffocating him. He wanted to close his eyes, to return to the warm sea of darkness. But there was something he had to do. . . .

Lyss! Where was Lyss? And why was it so dark? He squinted, shook his head, tried to push himself up. Something held him. He fumbled at his waist to release the seat belt, surprised by the weakness in his hands. Awkwardly, he ripped off his gloves and tossed them aside.

Lifting his head, he saw the immense dark hull of a truck crushed against the right side

159

of the car. Then he remembered. *The semi!* He tore the seat belt from his body and scrambled toward Lyss. The pain that ripped through his head at the sudden movement made him reel backward and fall against the seat. He squeezed his eyes shut once, pulled in a deep breath, then moved again, more carefully this time, reaching for her as he moved.

"Lyss . . . honey . . ."

He touched her hand, felt a sticky wetness on his fingers.

Blood . . . Lyss's blood . . .

He pulled at her seat belt, ignoring the pain in his head. He had to free her, had to get her out of the car. He couldn't bring himself to look at her. He fixed his eyes on the seat belt, forcing himself not to look at Lyss.

"It's OK, babe. . . . I'll have you out of here in a minute. You'll be all right. You'll be fine, babe. . . ."

Glass . . . there was glass everywhere . . . on the floor, on the seat, on her lap, her hands, her arms. . . . So much glass. . . .

She made a terrible sound, a wheezing, choking sound as though she were fighting for breath. Finally, the belt was free. He forced himself to look up. There was so much glass . . . so much blood. . . .

Again Lyss choked, an awful strangling noise. Gabe felt dizzy, then sick. "Lyss . . ."

Out of the darkness, he heard an engine coming toward them. It slowed, then stopped. In the gleam of the headlights, Gabe saw her face . . . his beautiful Lyss . . . shattered like a broken mirror. . . .

In that instant he could almost hear the sound of his own heart breaking and shattering into pieces.

FOURTEEN

After Gabe and Lyss left, Jennifer took the children upstairs to bed. When she checked an hour later, she found all three asleep. Jason and Nicky had gallantly given the bed to Stacey and her doll. Sunny lay on the floor beside the bed, her eyes following Jennifer as she tiptoed around the room.

After watching them for a moment more, Jennifer gave Sunny a pat on the head, extinguished the small oil lamp on the bedside table, and went back downstairs.

Daniel and Teddy Giordano were sitting in the kitchen where she had left them. A lamp flickered softly in the middle of the table. In its glow, the men's faces were lined with fatigue and worry.

"We should try to get some sleep," Jennifer suggested halfheartedly. Teddy looked at her and shrugged, while Daniel nodded distractedly, saying nothing.

Earlier she had closed the kitchen curtains. Now she walked to the window, pulled one panel to the side, and looked out.

Snow and ice glazed the window, but she could see that the snow was still falling, could hear the wind wailing. With a sigh, she dropped the curtain and went to sit on the bench beside Daniel.

He covered her hand with his. "Why don't you go lie down for a while?"

"It would be useless. I can't even *sit* still, much less lie down."

"They'll be all right, Jennifer."

"It's such an awful night. . . ."

"Gabe could drive that Cherokee in his sleep," he pointed out.

"But the roads must be almost impassable. . . ."

"Honey —"

"I'm sorry." She took in a deep breath. "How long do you think they'll be gone?"

He shook his head. "It takes half an hour to get to Elkins in good weather. In this . . ." He left his sentence unfinished. "Did you hear something?"

Jennifer looked at him.

"I thought I heard a car."

Jennifer stood, then went back to the window and looked out, staring into the darkness. "Maybe Gabe couldn't get through," she said.

Teddy Giordano came to join her at the window. "I don't see any lights."

163

"Must have been an airplane," said Daniel. "I don't hear anything now. Jennifer, is there any coffee left?"

"No, but I'll make some," Jennifer said, glad for something to do.

Daniel pushed back from the table. "I'd better go up and check on the kids again."

"I was just upstairs, Daniel," Jennifer reminded him.

"Let me go," Teddy offered. "I need to stretch my legs anyway."

As Teddy left the room, Daniel came up behind Jennifer at the stove. "I wish you'd go to bed," he said, slipping his arms around her waist.

Jennifer turned to face him. "I can't, Daniel. Not until Gabe and Lyss get back."

He nodded, lightly resting his chin on top of her head.

Jennifer wished she could shake the growing knot of apprehension that had plagued her throughout the evening. "Lyss was worried, Daniel. I could tell."

His arms tightened around her. He said nothing but pressed a light kiss into her hair. Jennifer buried her face in the warmth of his sweater for another moment, wondering if the night would ever end.

Both of them jumped, startled, when they heard the sound of stamping feet on the deck. Upstairs, Sunny barked once, then again, as someone began to pound loudly on the door.

"They *are* back," Jennifer said, slipping quickly from Daniel's arms.

"Jennifer, wait —"

But Jennifer was already opening the door. "What happened, couldn't you —"

She stopped, staring blankly at the three men on the other side of the door.

The one standing in front of the others was thin and pale, but neatly dressed in an obviously expensive topcoat. Behind him, a bearded middle-aged man, with a coat hanging loosely on his gaunt frame, stood watching her. The third man was moderately tall and broad-shouldered in a dark leather jacket; he had thinning hair and a dark mustache. Snow clung to them, and they looked extremely cold.

"Excuse us, ma'am." The man in the well-cut topcoat spoke first. "We were wondering if we could use your phone? I'm afraid we're hung up in a snowdrift." He rubbed his gloved hands together and craned his neck to look past Jennifer into the cabin.

Daniel had come to stand beside her. "What's the problem?" he asked, putting his hand on Jennifer's arm.

"We're really sorry to bother you," the apparent spokesman of the group said, smiling pleasantly. "We must have taken a wrong turn somewhere. We got about halfway down the road leading in here before we realized we were lost. Then we got stuck in a drift and had to walk the rest of the way." He stopped, extending his hand to Daniel. "Jay Wolf here," he said amiably.

Daniel merely inclined his head, saying nothing. The other's expression darkened, and he dropped his hand to his side.

Jennifer's uneasiness grew as she watched the man's peculiar pale eyes narrow to a cold stare. "I'm sorry," she said, wanting only to be rid of these strangers, "but our phone —"

Daniel stopped her, his grasp tightening on her arm. "Where exactly were you headed?"

"Actually, we're looking for some friends of ours who live in the area. It's just that we don't know this part of the country, and the storm has made it nearly impossible to find their . . . farm."

"If they live around here," Daniel answered shortly, "I'm sure we know them. What are their names?"

Irritation flared in the man's eyes. "Can't we just use your phone?"

166

Daniel hesitated only an instant. "I'm afraid we can't help you." As he spoke, he released Jennifer's arm and reached for the door.

It happened so fast, Jennifer was never sure who made the first move. Teddy came back into the room, and she heard him choke off an exclamation behind her. At the same time, the man in the topcoat pulled a handgun. His hard kick at the door sent it slamming against the wall as he and the other two men came charging into the kitchen, guns drawn.

"Jennifer —" Daniel reached for her, but the muscular man in the leather jacket stopped him.

"Move back, big guy — against the wall."

When Daniel didn't react, he rammed the pistol hard into his stomach. "I said *move back! Now!*"

"Stop it!" Jennifer screamed at him. "He can't see you! He's blind!"

All three men froze, their eyes locking on Daniel. But only for an instant. Almost immediately, their attention went to Teddy Giordano, who now stood in the middle of the room, his face a taut, angry mask.

"Well, well . . ." The man with the cold eyes took a step toward Teddy, then stopped, his gun leveled at him. "Will you look who's become a country boy."

Jennifer shuddered at the wide, toothy smile, the feral expression that suggested an underlying viciousness.

"You've been bad, Teddy-boy. Very bad." Still smiling darkly, the man in the topcoat closed the distance between them.

Teddy stood rigid and unmoving. Jennifer saw his hands clench into tight fists at his sides as he met the other's gaze with a defiant stare.

For a moment, they stood staring at each other in silence. It was Teddy who spoke first. "What do you want, Wolf?"

The man called Wolf smirked, then laughed — a high, almost shrill hacking sound that struck Jennifer as strangely obscene.

Abruptly, the man's expression sobered. His pale eyes watered as he fixed a contemptuous glare on Teddy Giordano. "What do we *want?*" He pressed a finger to the side of his nose and sniffed. "You know what we want, Teddy-boy. We want Nick's notebook." He sniffed again, then added, "And we'd also like to have a little talk with the kids."

"I don't know anything about any notebook, Wolf. Or the kids."

Wolf's eyes never left Teddy's face.

"None of that, Teddy-boy. Don't lie to me. I hate it when people lie to me. I'm going to have the notebook. And I'm going to talk with the kids. That's what we're here for." Without warning, his gaze went to Jennifer. "In the meantime, why don't you introduce us to your new friends?"

Teddy looked at Jennifer, and his eyes seemed to plead for forgiveness. Then he turned back to Wolf. "This is between us, Wolf. Leave them out of it."

Wolf let his watery gaze play slowly over Jennifer, then Daniel.

Finally, he turned back to Teddy. "You're in a lot of trouble, Teddy-boy," he said, again smirking. "Kidnapping is bad business. Very bad."

Teddy shot him a startled look. "Kidnapping! What are you talking about?"

Wolf shrugged, tipping his gun to Teddy's chin. "Nabbing two kids that don't belong to you —" He shook his head in a gesture of mock regret. "That's kidnapping, Teddy. The feds are looking for you, boy. You'd better let us help you."

Teddy blanched, but his expression never wavered. "I don't know what you're talking about."

Wolf's smile faded. "OK, punk. You want to play games? We'll play *my* games."

His eyes still locked on Teddy, he snapped out orders to the other two men. "Arno, take the woman in the other room and tie her up."

As the broad-shouldered man in the leather jacket took a step toward Jennifer, Daniel uttered an exclamation of anger and moved.

"Boone, keep that gun on the blind man!" snapped Wolf.

The hunched, older man moved in closer to Daniel, his gun wavering slightly.

Jennifer gasped as the man called Arno dug a gun into her side. "Let's go, lady."

"Leave her alone!" As accurately as if he could see the man's arm, Daniel struck out with one large hand and knocked the other man's gun free, sending it skating across the kitchen floor.

Furious, Arno hurled himself at Daniel, poised to slug him.

Jennifer screamed, and Boone moved in with his gun between Arno and Daniel. "Stop it, Chuck! Didn't you hear her? He's blind. He can't even see you!"

"That's enough!" Wolf shouted. "Get your gun, Chuck! And this time hold on to it."

He motioned Teddy against the wall with the others. "Get over there, Giordano."

When Teddy hesitated, Wolf shoved the gun against his ribs and growled, *"Now!"*

Teddy went to stand next to Daniel, whose face looked as if it had been carved from granite.

Wolf stepped up to them. "You don't look blind, mister," he snarled, tapping the barrel of his gun against Daniel's chest. "And you move pretty good for someone who can't see."

When Daniel remained stonily silent, Wolf turned his attention to Jennifer. She went weak with revulsion as she saw his expression change to a predatory stare. Her breath lodged in her throat, and she cringed, digging her hands into her sides so hard that pain shot up her arms.

"You're the blind man's lady?" Again, the ugly, chilling smile.

Jennifer nodded, trying desperately to look at something — anything — other than the man's face. "I'm his wife," she choked out.

One pale hand snaked out to capture her chin, forcing Jennifer to look at him. "His wife?"

Again she nodded, squeezing her eyes shut against the cold touch of his skin against her face.

Unexpectedly, he dropped his hand.

"Then I suggest," he said softly, "that you convince him to be a good boy and do exactly what he's told. And I suggest that you do the same."

Jennifer shuddered at the corruption she could feel emanating from the man. It was almost as if she could sense his evil seeping through her own skin.

He's insane, her mind clamored. *He's insane . . . and . . . deadly.*

Suddenly the man seemed to lose interest in her, transferring his attention back to Teddy. "Where are the kids?" he barked.

Teddy didn't look at him. "Pittsburgh, I suppose," he snapped.

Wolf sneered and struck the younger man, hard, across the face. "I *said* . . . where are the kids?"

Teddy glared at him with undisguised fury but remained grimly silent.

"You're making me very angry, Teddy-boy," Wolf said mildly. "I should think by now you'd know it's a mistake to make me angry." He glanced at Daniel, his mouth twisting into a derisive smile. "Now then, punk," he said, still watching Daniel's face, "you're going to tell me where the Angelini brats are, or I'm going to put a bullet between the blind man's eyes." With an ugly, teasing motion, he turned the gun on Daniel and mimed the act of shooting him.

Jennifer cried out, but Wolf ignored her, now training the gun on Teddy.

A ring of sweat banded Teddy's forehead. He looked from Wolf to Daniel, then back to the man with the gun. Finally, his voice ragged with defeat, he said, "They're upstairs." He moistened his lips. "Wolf, leave them alone! They don't know anything!"

Wolf ignored him. "Get upstairs," he said, glancing at the tall, bearded man. "Stay with the kids."

His gun still on Teddy, he turned to Arno. "I *said* take the woman out of here and tie her up. Do it now." He inclined his head toward the doorway into the great room, adding, "In there. And watch her close." He smiled his chilling smile. "She looks like trouble to me."

Jennifer felt the blood drain from her face. Her entire body began to shake when Arno jabbed her with the gun. "You heard him, lady. Move it."

"Jennifer —"

She saw Daniel lunge as if to charge toward her, then stop when Wolf pressed the tip of the gun barrel to the side of his head.

"Sit down, blind man! And shut up! Or

I'm going to make your woman a widow!"

Jennifer stole one last look at Daniel, his face white and lined with fury, as the two men prodded her out of the kitchen.

FIFTEEN

The great room that had earlier seemed so cozy to Jennifer now appeared eerie and forbidding in the flickering glow of the oil lamps and the dying embers in the fireplace.

The man called Arno looked around the room, then turned to his partner. "Where's the upstairs in this —"

At that moment a door above them opened, and his words were lost in the sudden din from the stairway. Sunny came roaring down the steps, snarling and barking furiously. She headed straight for Arno.

Standing behind Jennifer, his gun shoved hard into her back, Arno jumped and yelled, instinctively turning the gun on the retriever.

"*No!*" Jennifer screamed, hurling herself in front of the dog. "Sunny — *no!*"

The retriever thundered to a dead stop, all four legs stiff and poised. Her eyes, dark with confusion and distrust, flicked from Jennifer to Arno, and she bared her teeth in a low, menacing growl.

"Sunny . . ." With great effort, Jennifer

kept her voice even and firm. "It's all right, Sunny." She turned to Arno. "Please, she's my husband's guide dog. Don't —"

A muffled sound from the top of the stairs made her whirl around.

"*Nicky!*" she cried out. "Go back inside the bedroom!"

The boy was poised at the top of the steps, staring down at Jennifer and the two men. Behind him, just beyond the bedroom door, stood Jason. He was holding Stacey's hand.

"Boone?" Nicky adjusted his glasses and peered down into the firelit great room. His gaze flicked from Boone to Arno, locking on the gun in the burly mobster's hand. "What are you guys doing here?" In the light from the fireplace, Jennifer could see the boy's face, hard and unexpectedly mature.

"Hey — Nicky!" Grinning, Boone started toward the stairs but stopped when Sunny's growl increased to a warning snarl.

"Mommy?" Jason's voice sounded small and uncertain. He led Stacey along beside him as he stepped closer to Nicky. The little girl rubbed at her eyes, staring down into the great room with a look of surprise. Her eyes widened when she saw the gun in Arno's hand.

The mobster grabbed Jennifer's arm from behind, again pushing the gun against her back. "Lady, you get that dog out of my way, or I'll blow her to bits!"

Jennifer swallowed hard, looking wildly from the retriever to the children standing at the top of the steps.

I mustn't panic. . . . Oh, Lord, don't let me panic.

"Jason . . ." Her voice was tremulous. She stopped, then began again. "Jason, call Sunny. Then I want you children to go into the bedroom, shut the door, and stay there. With Sunny. Do you understand?"

The boy looked at her, then at Arno and Boone. "Where's Daddy?"

"He's in the kitchen with Teddy . . . and another man. He's all right, Jason. Now, please, honey — do as I say."

"Who are *they?*" Jason asked.

Helplessly, Jennifer looked at Nicky.

Nicky glared at Boone with disgust. "Wolf's in the kitchen, right? With Teddy? You guys are here to finish what you started with Papa, I suppose."

Boone's face sagged with a wounded expression. "No, Nicky," he whined, shaking his head. "We just need to talk to you and Teddy. Teddy's got something that belongs to Mr. Sabas."

Nicky didn't take his eyes off the man as he said, "Jason, do what your mother said. Call Sunny."

Jason moved a few steps into the landing, then stopped. "Sunny — come on, girl!"

The retriever turned and looked up the stairs, then back to Jennifer, her eyes uncertain.

Again, Jason called her. This time, she hesitated only an instant before sprinting up the steps.

"Go back to the bedroom, Jason," Nicky told him. "Take Sunny and Stacey with you."

Responding to the tone of authority in Nicky's voice, Jason again glanced down the steps. When Jennifer gave him a small nod, he turned and led Stacey back to the bedroom. The retriever followed obediently.

"Get upstairs with those kids," Arno growled at Boone. "And *stay* up there with them, you understand?"

As Jennifer watched, Boone hesitated, glancing from Arno up to Nicky. He put his gun away before starting to shuffle up the steps.

"Better keep your gun handy if you're coming up here to *guard* us, Boone," Nicky sneered, folding his arms across his chest. "An unarmed man wouldn't have a chance against three dangerous kids like us."

"Hey, come on, Nicky," Boone said peevishly. "You know old Boone wouldn't lay a hand on you or your sister. We just want to talk to you, that's all."

Nicky pushed his glasses up with one finger, then leveled a scathing look of contempt at the man on the steps. "Talk about what, Boone? How you killed Papa? What you're going to do to Teddy . . . and to us?"

By the time he reached the landing, Boone was gasping for breath. "Now, you just hush that kind of talk, Nicky!" he muttered defensively, wheezing hard. "I told you, Teddy has something that belongs to Mr. Sabas. We just came to get it back. No one's gonna hurt you or your sister."

"Cut the gab and get those kids in the bedroom!" Arno shouted up the steps. "And *keep* them there, you hear?"

"Come on, Nicky. We'd better do like he says," Boone grumbled.

The boy glared at him with a mixture of anger and contempt. "Still letting Rambo rattle your chain, huh, Boone?"

"Nicky —" Boone glanced back at Arno.

Nicky ignored him. "Don't let him scare you, Mrs. Kaine," he said, glaring down the stairway at Arno. "He thinks he's a real tough guy, but he has the backbone of a slug."

Arno scowled up at the boy but said nothing. After Nicky and Boone finally disappeared into the bedroom, he jabbed his gun into Jennifer's ribs. "Get over to the couch," he told her, his voice rough. He motioned for her to sit down; then, keeping his gun trained on her, he reached inside his jacket and withdrew a twist of rope.

"You don't have to tie me up," Jennifer said, wincing at the tremor in her voice. "I'm not likely to make any trouble, not when someone has a gun trained on my husband and my son."

As if he hadn't heard her, he laid the gun on the table beside the couch. "Put your hands behind your back," he ordered her.

Jennifer hesitated, and he pushed at her with one hand. "Lady, just *do* it!"

Arno bound her hands, then trussed her ankles together as well. Straightening, he retrieved the gun and glanced around the room. "What kind of place is this, anyway?" he asked Jennifer. "You guys farmers or what?"

She shook her head. "It's a camp. For disabled children," she said tonelessly.

His lip curled with distaste. "*Handicapped* kids? A camp for cripples?"

Jennifer stared at him incredulously, for

an instant too shocked to answer. "They're not . . . *cripples!*" she finally managed to choke out. "They're children. Disabled children."

He looked at her with open disgust. "What's with you, anyway? You're married to a blind man, working in a camp for crippled kids — you got something against *normal* people?" He paused, moving in closer to her. "I bet there's something wrong with *you*, too, huh? Maybe something you try to keep a secret. Something that doesn't show, right?"

Another madman, she thought wildly. She squeezed her eyes shut. He was so close she could hear the rasp of his breath, could smell some kind of sickeningly sweet hairgrooming product, could feel his small cold eyes on her.

Unexpectedly, he moved away and started walking around the room. "Who else is here besides you and the others? Anyone?"

Jennifer hesitated. She was relieved that Gabe and Lyss hadn't been trapped in this nightmare with them, yet she half wished they were here. Two more adults might have made a difference.

"I said, who else is here?" He scowled at her.

"No one." The words were lost in a rising

wave of panic. Jennifer forced a note of calm into her voice. "No one else. The couple who manages the camp are on vacation. We're just filling in for them while they're away."

"You got a phone here, don't you?" His gaze scanned the room, locking on the wall phone.

"It's . . . out of order," Jennifer told him. "The storm . . ."

"Yeah, it's a real monster, ain't it?"

Jennifer had a sudden, irrational urge to laugh. Here she was, tied up and held captive by a gunman; Jason was locked upstairs with an aging thug; and Daniel — her throat closed with sick fear — Daniel was the prisoner of a lunatic. And all the while she was expected to make small talk with this . . . *gorilla?*

"How long have Giordano and the kids been here, anyway?"

She looked at him. "I . . . I'm not sure."

Again, he moved closer to her, his posture aggressive as he rolled the gun around his hand almost casually. "You're not real smart, are you, sweetheart? What a pair, a blind man and a dummy," he said scornfully. "You're a looker, though," he added, sounding almost surprised.

The warmth from the fire suddenly

seemed to disappear, and Jennifer shivered.

"What's a classy chick like you doin' hooked up with a blind man?"

When she neither answered nor met his gaze, he moved even closer. As if to deliberately intimidate her, he kept the gun trained on her while with the other hand he lifted a strand of her hair, then let it tumble slowly over his fingertips.

Jennifer flinched and twisted her head to one side.

He laughed. "Nervous, are you? Relax, sweetheart. It could be a very long night."

Jennifer felt a wave of nausea sweep through her as he looked at her for a moment, then put his gun down and shrugged out of his jacket. "It's getting warm in here," he said with a leer. "Might as well get comfortable — we're going to be here for a while."

Daniel's apprehension mounted as he listened to the two men at the kitchen table. Seated beside Teddy on the harvest bench for what seemed like hours, he could sense the tension in the younger man.

"Stall as long as you like, Teddy-boy," the man called Wolf said, his voice smooth. "I'm in no particular hurry to go back outside. I'm going to get what I came for eventually, but we can play games for a little longer, if you want."

"I'm not playing games, Wolf," Teddy said, his voice low and tight. "I told you, I don't have any notebook. And those kids know *nothing* about Nick's business. You know he always kept his family out of it. He even shut *me* out."

"Oh, I'm not worried about what the kids know about Nick's business, Teddy-boy. I'm only interested in what they know about Nick's — *execution.*"

When Teddy made no reply, Wolf went on in the same casual, unhurried tone. "You see, some people might get the wrong idea about Nick's death. If they listened to just anyone, they might even suspect that his friends had something to do with it. Or even someone in the *Family.*"

Daniel heard the chair creak as the mobster got up and began to pace the room.

"Now, we wouldn't want anyone coming to the wrong conclusions about the Family, would we, Teddy-boy? So if Nick's kids have any information at all about who might have murdered their papa, we need to know. Understand?"

"I already *told* you — the kids don't know anything!"

Teddy's voice was strained as he pushed

away from the table with a thud. "Don't you have any feelings at all?" he grated out. "They're just kids, Wolf!" He stopped, then added, "Kids without *parents*."

"Sit down, punk. I'll tell you when you can get up." Wolf's tone went hard. "I think maybe you don't understand how serious this is. This is important, Teddy-boy. *Extremely* important." He paused, and when he went on, there was no mistaking the threat in his words. "I want the notebook, Teddy-boy. I want it now."

When Teddy tried to interrupt, Wolf slammed his hand down on the table.

"Otherwise," Wolf went on, his voice softer but even more menacing, "maybe I can convince your blind friend here to persuade you."

"Wolf —"

"Shut up, Teddy-boy." Wolf's tone was still deceptively quiet. "Better yet," he continued, "maybe I can convince his *wife* to help us out."

Daniel's pent-up rage finally exploded. He tilted the harvest table with both hands and let it slam back to the floor. "Don't you *touch* her!" he roared, jumping to his feet.

"Sit *down*, blind man!" Wolf shouted. "*Now!* I don't think you understand what's

185

going on here. I'll do whatever I please. *I've got the control!* Now sit down and shut up!"

Daniel heard the safety of the gun click only a second before Teddy grabbed his arm.

"Dan, do what he says! He's just crazy enough to shoot you!"

For a moment every fiber of Daniel's body seemed coiled to its limit, stretched beyond endurance. Finally, he sank back onto the bench, a mixture of defeat and helplessness washing over him in one enormous, crushing wave.

Merciful Lord, don't let him touch Jennifer. . . . Don't let these animals hurt her.

He started in surprise at Teddy's next words. "All right, Wolf. I'll give you the notebook."

There was a long silence. "I thought you'd come around, Teddy-boy," said Wolf, "once you understood how important it is to us."

"But it's not here," Teddy added. "I hid it."

"Where?" Daniel heard the suspicious snap in the mobster's voice.

"It's in one of the barns. At the other end of the camp."

Wolf softly rapped the table with what sounded like the butt of the gun. "If you're lying to me, Teddy-boy," he said softly, "you won't get a second chance. I'll line you and everyone else in this cabin up against the wall and start shooting. Do you understand me?"

"I'm not lying," Teddy answered woodenly.

"I hope not, kid." There was another moment of silence. "All right," Wolf said. "Both of you, stay put. I'm going to talk to Arno a minute, and then we'll go get the notebook."

He stopped, sniffed once, then again. "Incidentally, blind man, the gun will be pointed at your head — so behave yourself."

Both Daniel and Teddy remained stonily quiet while the other men carried on a hurried exchange between the two rooms.

". . . I'm taking the blind man with us." Wolf's speech was fast now, his tone sharp and authoritative. Daniel had the distinct feeling that the man's next words were emphasized for his and Teddy's benefit. "You go up and tell Boone what's going on, and make sure he understands. If I'm not back here within an hour, have him take care of those kids." He paused. "And you take care of the woman."

Then he turned his attention back to Teddy and Daniel. "All right, punk. Get a coat for yourself and the blind man."

Daniel heard Teddy leave and return a moment later. "I need my dog if I'm going outside," he said as he slipped into the bomber jacket Teddy handed him.

Wolf uttered a groan of disgust. "Teddy-boy can be your guide dog, blind man! Now, *move!*" Without warning, he cracked Daniel across the back of the neck with the handle of the gun.

Daniel's knees buckled as a fireball of pain shot through him. He staggered and lunged forward, almost falling.

Teddy grabbed for his arm, steadying him as he led him through the outside door.

"Let up on him, Wolf," he grated angrily. "He's *blind!*"

"He's going to be *dead* if the two of you don't get moving."

"Let's go, Dan. The sooner I give them what they want, the sooner they get out of your life."

"You know better than that," Daniel muttered.

"Listen, Dan — just do what he says," Teddy whispered, his tone urgent. "Whatever you do, don't provoke him."

Outside, the snow had tapered to little more than a fine mist. Daniel slipped once, stumbling over a rock. Teddy caught him.

"Wolf, this is crazy. Let him stay inside."

Wolf's only reply was to jab the gun even harder into Daniel's lower back.

"Dan . . ." Teddy whispered as he clutched Daniel's arm, guiding him through the deep snow. "Dan . . . I know it doesn't help, but I'm sorry. . . . I'm so sorry for what I've done to you and your family."

His head still ringing from the blow in the kitchen, Daniel could only nod and go on.

SIXTEEN

Jason couldn't quite make up his mind about the man called Boone. He didn't have the same . . . *bad* look in his eyes that the other two men did. Yet Nicky seemed to be really angry with him, apparently because of something to do with his "papa."

Jason had never heard anyone call his daddy "papa" before. Maybe that was the kind of word *geniuses* used. He had heard Teddy talking to Uncle Gabe and Daddy about Nicky, explaining how Nicky was a *genius*. Apparently, being a genius meant you were different from other kids, because Nicky attended a special kind of school, too. Jason didn't think he was a genius like Nicky, but he knew all about being different.

Right now, though, Nicky looked just like any other kid who was angry with someone. He was frowning at the tall thin man, and he looked really fierce.

Jason held on to Stacey's hand as he listened to Nicky and Boone.

"I didn't have nothing to do with hurting

your papa, Nicky. I wouldn't have laid a hand on Nick. No way."

Nicky pushed his glasses up a notch, staring up into Boone's face. "I know that," he said impatiently. "It was Wolf. Wolf and Arno."

The man stiffened, taking a step back from the boy. "How'd you know that?"

Nicky didn't answer but simply continued to watch Boone.

"Whatever you do, boy, don't let on to them that you know anything," Boone warned him in a gruff voice. "Now listen, Nicky, you tell me the truth. *Were* you in the house? Did you hear what went on the day your papa . . . the day he died?"

"Why do you want to know, Boone?"

Jason watched, fascinated, as the man swallowed. Boone's neck was extremely long and skinny, with a lump at the bottom that rose and fell every time he swallowed or even took a deep breath.

"Nicky, honest now — I'm tellin' you the truth! The only reason we're here is to get that notebook that belongs to the Boss — Mr. Sabas — and to make sure you and Stacey get back home safe. That's all there is to it, and you're just gonna make trouble for you and your little sister if you don't do what Wolf tells you."

Nicky's only reply was a sneer.

Boone glanced over his shoulder at the closed door, then moved closer to Nicky. He stooped down and lowered his voice. "Listen to me, Nicky. If you —" His eyes went to Stacey for a minute. "If you or your sister heard anything that went on at the house the day . . . your papa died, don't admit it."

Jason saw with surprise that Nicky's eyes had suddenly filled with tears.

"You were there that day, weren't you, Boone?" Nicky asked quietly. "You and Arno . . . and Wolf."

The man shook his head. "I wasn't! I swear to you, Nicky, I *wasn't!*" He looked away, then back to Nicky. "I was in the car. I didn't know anything until it was over. Arno told me later. That's the truth, boy. That's the truth."

He straightened, coughed, and went on. "Your papa did something he shouldn't have done, Nicky. He tried to get the Boss — and the Family — in trouble." Again he shook his head. "He shouldn't have done that."

"So Wolf killed him," Nicky said flatly. "And now he's going to kill Teddy. And maybe Stacey and me, too."

"No!" Boone laughed, but Jason could

tell it wasn't a happy laugh — it was strained, as if it hurt Boone's throat to get it out. "Why would he kill Teddy? Wolf likes Teddy, you know that. We *all* like Teddy!" He grinned at Nicky. "For a kid who's supposed to be so smart, you sure got a lot of crazy ideas, you know that?"

Nicky stared up at him for a long time. The room was quiet, except for Sunny's shallow breathing.

Finally Nicky spoke. "*You* guys are the crazy ones, if you really think Teddy has that notebook." An odd little smile broke across his face as he watched Boone's reaction to his words.

"What?" The man's voice was gruff. "What do you mean?"

Still smiling, Nicky said, "I heard Arno talking to you out in the hall a few minutes ago. About Teddy and Wolf going to find the notebook." He squinted at Boone. "But *I'm* the one who hid the notebook, not Teddy."

Boone had straightened up, but he stooped down again. It must have hurt, because Jason saw him make a face as if he was in pain. He took Nicky by the shoulders and shook him a little. "Don't you lie about this, boy!"

Sunny growled and rose to her feet. Jason,

too, stepped forward. He wasn't sure what he could do, but he wanted to help Nicky. Boone straightened again, holding up both hands, palms outward, as if to show that he meant no harm to Nicky.

Jason told Sunny to stay, and the dog settled down beside him, still alert and watching quietly.

"What about the notebook, Nicky?" Boone asked, his eyes on Sunny.

"Do you think Papa would have trusted anyone but me with that notebook?" Nicky said softly. He had an expression in his eyes that Jason didn't understand — like he knew some kind of secret he wasn't telling.

Boone shook his head. "Then why did Teddy run off with you kids the way he did? And why did he tell Wolf he had the notebook?"

"To protect us," the boy said, emphasizing each word as if he were the adult and Boone the child. "Teddy knows Wolf too well. He was trying to get him away from us."

Boone's eyes narrowed. "Are you tellin' me the truth, Nicky?"

The boy nodded, his gaze steady.

"What do you think Wolf's gonna do when he finds out Teddy lied to him?" Boone rubbed his beard and frowned.

Nicky's voice sounded hard and cold when he answered. "Wolf's going to kill Teddy no matter what. We both know that." Jason saw that same secret kind of smile spread across Nicky's face. "Unless we stop him."

"Stop him?" Boone's chin trembled, but he looked interested.

Nicky nodded. "If I were to give *you* the notebook before Wolf finds out what Teddy's up to, do you think you could convince Wolf not to hurt Teddy — or us?"

Boone looked from Nicky to Stacey, licking his lips. Finally he said, "Yeah. Sure." He nodded. "Sure, I could. Wolf would be so happy I got the notebook for him, he'd listen to me. Where is it?"

Nicky blinked, then said evenly, "It's not in *here*, Boone. I'm smarter than that." He nodded, and Jason thought he looked pleased. "It's in a safe place. No one but me is ever going to find that notebook."

Boone scratched his head.

"Listen, Boone, I'll take you to it. We'll get that notebook before Wolf finds out that Teddy lied to him." He stopped, lowering his voice even more. "But you've got to promise me that you won't let Wolf or that creep, Arno, hurt us."

Boone put a hand on the boy's shoulder.

"Hey, Nicky — you've got my word." He pressed his thin lips together in a worried expression. "But how are we gonna get the notebook? Chuck's right downstairs underneath us with the woman. And I'm supposed to stay with you kids 'til Wolf gets back."

Nicky pulled his mouth to one side and pushed his glasses up on his nose. He looked at Jason and Stacey, then back up at Boone. "I know what we can do," he finally said, his tone firm. "We'll just have to tell Arno the truth. Now, here's what we'll do, Boone. You go downstairs and explain to Arno about the notebook. Tell him where we're going, and that Jason and Stacey will have to stay with him. Then you and I will go after the notebook."

Boone cocked his head to one side and scratched his chin. "Yeah," he said slowly. "Arno won't stop us, once he knows where we're goin'."

He glanced at Sunny. "I don't know about that dog, though." He gave Nicky a nasty grin. "He'd shoot me for sure if he knew I told anyone, but Arno is scared to death of dogs," he whispered to Nicky.

Nicky laughed with him. "We'll take Sunny with us. Hey, she can even help us dig."

"No," Jason argued uneasily, beginning to feel angry with Nicky. "Sunny won't go with you unless I tell her to. And I'm not going to tell her to. She's supposed to stay here with us." He suddenly felt very frightened. There was nothing familiar or safe in this room except Sunny.

Boone frowned at him. Jason stepped back but continued to watch the man.

"Now listen here, kid, we don't have time to waste. We're gonna go get that —"

"Wait a minute, Boone," Nicky interrupted, tugging at his sleeve. "You go on down and explain things to Arno. Let me talk to Jason a minute, OK?"

Boone studied him. "Well . . . all right," he finally said. "But the dog will have to go with us. You get your coat on and be ready."

Nicky stood watching Boone shuffle stiffly out of the bedroom. Then he hurried across the room to bolt the door.

Puzzled, Jason watched him. "What are you doing?"

The other boy turned around, his back to the locked door. He put a finger to his lips, cautioning Jason and Stacey to be quiet. His eyes looked like black coals as he looked from Jason to his sister.

"Why did you lock the door?" Jason asked.

Nicky smiled. "I'm eliminating some of their ammunition," he said.

"Am-ammunition?" Jason repeated with a frown.

Nicky left the door and quickly crossed the room. "Wolf would have used *us* to get what he wanted from Teddy — or from your parents," he explained. "He wouldn't think twice about shooting all three of us if it would help him."

"How do you know so much about these men?"

"They work . . . for the same people my papa worked for," Nicky said. "They used to be at our house a lot. I got to know them pretty well."

Jason knew he might not like the answer, but he had to ask the question. "They're not good men, are they?"

Nicky shook his head, taking Stacey's hand when she came to stand beside him. "No, they're not," he said without hesitation. "Boone's probably the best of the three, but that's not saying much. Lucky for us, he's not too bright. The one downstairs — Chuck Arno — he's not a whole lot smarter than Boone, but he can get mean. He's kind of weird, you know? Thinks everything has to be perfect or it's no good."

He stopped and glanced down at Stacey. She still looked scared, but she smiled a little.

"Wolf is the dangerous one," Nicky went on. "Wolf is smart. Maybe as smart as I am," he said matter-of-factly. "But my papa said that Wolf's brain is probably rotten by now, from all the drugs he's done."

He pulled Stacey more tightly to his side. "Being around Wolf always makes me feel kind of . . . creepy. I think he likes to hurt people. I mean, really *likes* it." He shook his head. "Wolf's the worst of them, that's for sure."

Jason's stomach felt funny. "What are we going to do now?"

Nicky didn't answer right away. His eyes went around the room as if he was looking for something. Finally he pointed at the tall, narrow window beside the bed. "What's outside that window?"

"Just a porch." Jason tried to remember what Mommy called it. "A . . . balcony."

Nicky's eyes brightened. "A balcony?" He dropped his hand from Stacey's shoulder and went quickly to the window. Without opening it, he peered outside for a minute.

When he turned back, he was smiling.

SEVENTEEN

Jason looked up from the ground at the support pole that ran from the balcony to the lower deck. He could understand why Sunny didn't want to jump. She was a *dog*. But why was Stacey making such a big deal out of it? There was a post all the way down. All she had to do was hang on and slide.

Nicky had already done it by throwing a pillowcase full of stuff over, then sliding down ahead of her. And Jason had done it, even though he wasn't a . . . a genius like Nicky.

Jason watched Stacey now and tried not to laugh. All three of them had pulled on jeans and coats over their pajamas. Stacey looked like an inner tube. She could hardly move. Jason didn't want to hurt her feelings by laughing at her, but she did look pretty funny.

Stacey glared down at her brother and Jason. "Let Sunny go first," she whispered, a little too loudly.

"Shh!" Nicky warned her. "They'll hear

us." He glanced around. "Jason, try to get Sunny to jump. Stacey won't stay up there by herself. If Sunny comes down, *she'll* come down."

But for the first time Jason could remember, Sunny refused to obey. Jason tried motioning with his hand, the way he had seen Daddy do. But Sunny just stared down at him without moving.

Jason planted his legs apart and spread his arms wide. He slipped in the snow and grabbed at Nicky to keep from falling. Opening his arms once more, he ordered as loudly as he dared, *"Sunny — come!"*

The retriever only cocked her head.

"Sunny doesn't want to jump," Stacey said. "She wants to stay here with me."

Jason didn't know what to do. He looked at Nicky for help.

Nicky studied both the dog and his sister for a moment. "Stacey, throw Mrs. Whispers down to me."

Stacey's face crumpled. "I *won't!*" she whispered back. Glaring down at him, she clutched the rag doll tightly against her.

"I'll catch her, Stacey, I promise. Just toss her down to me. Come on. You'll see why in a minute."

Stacey gave her brother one more look — a scrunched-up pout Jason thought was probably her "mean look" — then carefully dropped her doll over the banister. Both she and Sunny watched Mrs. Whispers fall into Nicky's arms.

As Nicky caught the doll, he said, "Now, Jason — call Sunny!" He looked up at his sister. "Stacey, help Sunny over the rail. Hurry!"

Jason was pretty sure that Stacey didn't trust what Nicky said anymore, but finally she stepped behind the retriever. Jason opened his arms. "Jump, Sunny!" he commanded in a harsh whisper. "Come on, jump!" The dog glanced from Jason to the doll in Nicky's arms, then at Stacey. Finally, she raised herself as much as possible on her hind legs, thrust her head forward, and pawed at the balcony rail.

"*Now*, Stacey," Nicky rasped. *"Push!"*

Stacey took a deep breath, twisted her face into a terrible scowl, and pushed at the retriever's back end until Sunny went over the edge with a yelp.

The dog hit both boys when she landed, sending them into a deep snowdrift. Sunny got up and shook herself hard, splattering snow all over Jason and Nicky. They looked at each other for a minute, then broke into a fit of muffled giggles.

While they were still climbing out of the

snowdrift, Stacey pushed herself over the railing and came sliding down the post. She didn't look too happy about it, Jason thought, but at least she did it. Nicky was pretty smart, all right. He had known Stacey wouldn't stay up there alone.

"Come on," Nicky said breathlessly, hauling himself up and pounding the snow off his coat. "We have to get away from here and go help Teddy and your dad."

He grabbed his sister's hand, and the three of them slogged through the snow with Sunny to hide behind the row of bushes that ringed the cabin.

"What about Mommy?" Jason whispered as they huddled down behind the shrubs.

Nicky looked at him. "You're right." He drew in a deep breath. "We have to get Boone and Arno out of the cabin."

"But how?"

Nicky pressed his lips together, looking away into the distance. When he finally spoke, his voice was so soft Jason could scarcely hear him. "When they realize we're gone, Arno's going to send Boone outside to look for us. If we can keep Boone from going back into the cabin, Arno will get antsy and come out, too. He has your mom tied up, so he won't worry about leaving her alone for a few minutes."

He stopped, looking soberly at Jason. "We'll have to take care of Boone *and* Arno." A funny look crossed his face. "Then we'll go after Wolf."

As Jason watched Nicky, he felt his stomach quiver. Nicky was really smart, and Jason wished he could think even half that fast. But did Nicky really think he was smart enough to outsmart three grown-ups — grown-ups with *guns?*

"All of them?" Jason asked apprehensively. "How?"

"One at a time." Nicky looked pretty sure of himself, and Jason tried not to be afraid. "We can do it. Boone won't be any problem. Arno —" He shrugged. "I'll just have to think of something when the time comes."

Jason was still worried. "Why did you bring that stuff?" He pointed to the big bandanna and the blue pillowcase Nicky had taken from the bedroom.

"You'll see," the other boy answered. "Stay down, now. We have to watch for Boone."

Crouching down out of the wind, they waited. After a minute or two, they heard a furious pounding upstairs.

"That's Boone," Nicky whispered, "trying to get back into the bedroom."

The window was still open, and they could hear Boone shouting and banging on the bedroom door. The uproar went on for another two or three minutes, then stopped.

After another minute, they heard voices coming from the great room. Angry voices. But they couldn't make out what they were saying.

Nicky motioned for the others to stay put, then crept out from the bushes and tiptoed up the steps onto the deck.

Jason held Stacey's hand as he watched Nicky press himself against the wall beside the window. When the muffled voices inside the room grew louder, Nicky sprinted across the deck and back to the bushes. "Boone's coming out! I'm going to hide beside the steps. When he gets about halfway down, I'll trip him. As soon as you see him fall, come and help me."

"But then what will we do?" Jason asked.

Nicky touched Jason's shoulder and grinned. "We'll take care of old Boone! Don't worry. Just trust me."

Jason swallowed hard and nodded. Then Nicky was gone, running back to the cabin steps. He reached under his coat as he ran, pulling out a belt. When he got to the steps, he crawled into the bushes at the side, crouching down low so he couldn't be seen.

Within seconds, the door opened, and Boone stepped out onto the deck, the snow crunching under his feet. Carrying his gun in one hand and gripping the porch railing with the other, he trudged over to the steps, then started down.

Jason held his breath as he watched Boone take one step at a time, looking back and forth around the yard as he descended. He was only two steps away from the bottom when Nicky's hand reached out and yanked his left foot out from under him.

With a startled cry, Boone went flying off the steps. His gun sailed out of his hand and landed several feet away. At the same time, Nicky jumped out of the bushes and hurled himself onto the man's back. Taking their cue, Jason and Stacey ran to help, followed by Sunny, who planted herself in front of Boone and lifted her lip in a silent snarl.

Boone was lying face down in the snow, apparently stunned. Nicky sat on his back, pulling Boone's arms behind him. "Help me tie him up! Hurry!" he whispered hoarsely.

Jason threw himself onto Boone, pressing his arms down as hard as he could. Nicky reached around and stuffed the bandanna into Boone's mouth, then pulled the pillowcase over his head.

"Stacey — hold his head down!" Nicky commanded, raising up just enough to pull out his belt.

Boone struggled, trying to get up. Stacey frowned at her brother for a second, then flung herself across the man's shoulders. She pushed down, forcing his head even deeper into the snow.

While Stacey and Jason held the mobster down, Nicky used his belt to bind Boone's hands behind his back.

"Come on, you guys — help me! We'll put him in the fruit cellar!"

Jason went around to the other side of Boone, and the two boys jerked the stunned man to his feet, pushing him across the yard toward the fruit cellar. Stacey followed, and every now and then Sunny gave a low growl from behind, as if she was warning Boone not to give them too much trouble.

The fruit cellar was pitch black and cold. They pushed Boone up against one wall, and on Nicky's instructions, Jason lifted the pillowcase up over the man's head. Nicky pulled out the bandanna and tied it into a gag before Boone could do anything except let out an angry grunt.

When Nicky seemed satisfied that Boone wasn't going anywhere, he grabbed the pillowcase and headed back outside. He held the door open for Jason and Stacey, then locked it with the wooden crossbar.

"What do we do now?" Jason whispered when they reached their hiding place in the bushes.

Nicky looked at him. "Now we take care of Arno."

EIGHTEEN

Gabe stepped down from the cab of the tow truck, waving his thanks to the driver who had given him a lift from town. The man had offered to turn off the main highway and try his luck on the narrow country road leading to the Farm. Even though the sturdy old wrecker could probably have made it through the snow-clogged lane without any difficulty, Gabe had insisted on walking the rest of the way. The man had already done enough, and besides, he needed some time alone before he faced the others with the news about Lyss.

With considerable effort he limped down the road toward the entrance gate. The road was heavily drifted, but the snow had finally stopped. The worst of the storm was probably over, although that was small comfort now.

As soon as he passed the weathered old barn and empty farmhouse that had once belonged to Yancey's Dairy, Gabe began to watch for light from the main cabin. He was almost halfway down the road before the darkened security lights reminded him of the power outage.

As he plugged along the snow-covered road, Gabe tried to think of anything other than Lyss. But even when he wasn't actively thinking about her, he was still fervently praying for her. He had prayed all the way into town, holding Lyss's blood-soaked form in the cab of the wrecker as he repeatedly thanked the Lord for the tow-truck driver.

The burly young man — "Tom" — apparently owned a small towing business consisting of only two wreckers. During storms like this, he had explained to Gabe, he and his other driver made a practice of being out and available, monitoring the emergency frequencies for news of accidents or stranded vehicles. There had been no word of Gabe and Lyss's accident, of course. He had merely come upon them by chance. "Just a lucky break," he'd said.

Gabe knew better. It hadn't been luck. If the wrecker hadn't shown up when it did, he might have had even worse news for the others waiting in the cabin.

Coolheaded and efficient, the wrecker driver had radioed for the police and an ambulance before even going to check the cab of the semi. Then, to Gabe's amazement and enormous gratitude, he had not only waited with him until the ambulance arrived, but had actually followed them to the hospital in Elkins. And there he had stayed, waiting with Gabe for word of Lyss's condition.

His final act of kindness had been to drive Gabe back to the Farm.

Gabe had been touched by the kindness of strangers before tonight, but never like this — and never when he had needed it more. When he had waved his thanks to the young tow truck driver, he'd felt as though he were saying good-bye to his guardian angel.

Idly, he wondered how Tom had felt, when he'd told him he was an answer to prayer.

Now, as he trudged through the snow on the way to the cabin, his mind replayed those hours at the hospital. It occurred to him that, if there had been worse times in his life than this night, he couldn't think of any.

He had spent the first hour at the hospital in a near daze, praying desperately for Lyss the entire time the doctors were checking his injuries, later pacing the deserted waiting room as Tom sat nearby, watching him. Occasionally one of them would question the admitting clerk for word on Lyss. By the time one of the emergency-room physicians — Dr. Kline — finally appeared, Gabe was almost incoherent. He was shaking so violently that the doctor made him sit down before he would even discuss Lyss's injuries.

"Mr. Denton, please — over here."

A surge of panic roared up through Gabe. "Lyss —"

"Your wife is still unconscious," Dr. Kline told him, waiting until Gabe sank down into the chair. "It's going to be another two or three hours before we have the test results back so we can give you any kind of a prognosis."

"But she's alive. . . ."

"Yes." Dr. Kline paused. "But I should tell you —"

"Can I see her? I have to see her! Please —"

"Soon," Dr. Kline said firmly. "She's being moved to intensive care right now. Someone will come and take you to her. But please understand, Mr. Denton, your wife won't know you're there. I'm afraid she's in . . . very serious condition."

Fear washed over Gabe, and he gripped the arms of the chair to steady himself. He was surprised to feel a light touch on his shoulder. "Easy, friend. God's in control now."

Gabe stared up at the young truck driver; he had almost forgotten about him. Tom smiled, and for some reason this unexpected kindness nearly undid Gabe. His eyes burned with tears, and his hands began to shake even harder.

"Mr. Denton, are you sure you're all right?" Dr. Kline asked, watching Gabe with concern. "Maybe we'd better take a closer look at *you*."

Gabe raised a hand. "No, I'm fine. I'm OK. Just . . . tell me about my wife. Please. How badly is she injured?" His eyes caught the doctor's and held his gaze. "I want the truth," he added.

The physician nodded briefly, then gave him a thorough description of Lyss's condition, explaining that she had a number of external injuries — cuts, lacerations, and abrasions — but that these were all "treatable."

The longer the doctor spoke, the worse it sounded.

"Her right arm is broken, and she has a compound fracture in her right leg, as well." Dr. Kline stopped when he saw Gabe wince. "Those will cause her some pain and discomfort," he admitted, "but, again,

213

they're treatable." He hesitated, and an un-readable expression passed over his face.

"What else?" Gabe asked, his throat tight.

The doctor sighed. "She has some frac-tured ribs, and I'm afraid that's creating a more serious problem."

Gabe pulled in a deep breath, waiting.

"One lung has been punctured. We've ap-plied drainage tubes for now. We'll watch it closely and in a few more hours do further x-rays to see if the lung is reexpanding. If it is, she won't need surgery."

"Do you think it *will* . . . reexpand?"

"It's too soon to tell. But I'm hopeful."

Gabe swallowed hard against the knot of anxiety in his throat. He could wait no longer to ask. "Her face . . ."

Dr. Kline nodded, watching him care-fully. "Yes," he said quietly, his eyes gentle with understanding. "Glass from the win-dow resulted in some facial lacerations. But we've removed all the glass, and she doesn't seem to have any nerve damage." He paused. "She will need some cosmetic sur-gery, but the cuts weren't as deep or as se-vere as we originally thought. Right now, that lung is our main concern."

Gabe looked away. Lovely Lyss . . . she had the face of a model. Perfect features, flawless bone structure, exquisite skin . . .

Oh, Lord . . . just let her live . . . please. I'll help her through all the rest. I'll love her through it, Lord. Nothing matters except her life. . . . Please, Lord, just let her live.

Again he struggled for a deep breath. "She was unconscious . . . ," he began, then lost his voice to a tremor that racked his entire body.

The doctor frowned, measuring him as if he expected him to collapse at any instant. He gave a brief nod. "Yes, and that may last awhile. She was in shock when you brought her in. Until I saw the x-rays, I thought she might have a ruptured spleen, but she doesn't. She has lost a lot of blood, however." He managed a tired smile. "We're working, Mr. Denton. We'll do our best for her, I promise you."

Gabe searched the doctor's eyes. "There's one thing I don't hear you saying."

Dr. Kline met his gaze. "You want to know if she's going to be all right."

Gabe waited, saying nothing, his pulse thundering in his ears.

The doctor hesitated. "I can't give you any guarantees. But you asked me for the truth, and I *am* trying to give you that. Your wife is in serious condition. She has sustained some life-threatening injuries, but prompt treatment can make a real difference. We're going to do everything we can to get her through this, and right now I feel that we have her fairly well stabilized. But I can't promise you anything. Not yet."

Gabe pressed a fist against his mouth. He squeezed his eyes shut for a moment, then opened them, ignoring the tears that threatened to spill over. "Thank you . . . for leveling with me."

He pulled in a long ragged breath, then abruptly asked, "The driver of the truck that hit us — how is he?"

The doctor's face brightened a little. "He's going to be just fine. He has a concussion and a broken collar bone, but he's doing nicely."

Gabe nodded. "That's good," he said softly. "Lyss will be glad for that. It wasn't his fault, you know. The road . . ." His words fell away.

No, it wasn't the truck driver's fault. The blame . . . all of it . . . belonged to someone else. Teddy Giordano, that low-life little hood who had sucked all of them into this nightmare — the blame was his.

A blast of white-hot rage roared up in him, a rage accompanied by a raw, unmitigated wave of hatred. He shook his head, as if to shake off the fury that threatened to send him over the edge. "Please," he said, his voice thick, "may I see her now?"

They allowed him only a few brief minutes with Lyss before insisting that he leave, but Gabe knew he would carry the memory with him for the rest of his life. Nothing could have prepared him for the sight of her, lying there as still as death, tubes running everywhere. Casts and splints and bandages . . . so many bandages, especially on her face.

He couldn't see much of her face — only her closed eyes and a bit of pale skin around her chin — and for just an instant he felt a shameful pang of relief. He *had* seen her face, in the headlights of the tow truck. And he would see it again and again, he thought, for years to come. His mind had photographed it in one stark, agonizing second, and the image was now an indelible part of his memory. He would never forget the wave of abject terror that had seized him until something deep inside his soul had cried out the reminder that the face still belonged to Lyss — his wife, his lovely, beloved Lyss. . . .

Now, as he crossed the yard and headed toward the cabin, Gabe shivered, not so much from the cold as from the impact of all that had happened during this long night. Suddenly he felt exhausted, physically and emotionally depleted. But the night wasn't over. A heavy weight of dread settled over his heart as he considered that, thanks to Teddy Giordano and his cronies, it might *never* be over.

NINETEEN

At the steps to the deck, Gabe took a deep breath and waited for the throbbing in his head to subside. Something above him, something . . . out of place . . . caught his attention. His eyes scanned the front of the cabin, the deck, the windows, then the second floor —

"Uncle Gabe!"

He heard the loud whisper at the same time his eye caught the open window upstairs. He whirled around to find Jason tugging urgently at his coat, then turned again to note the curtain billowing in and out of the upstairs window.

Jason grabbed his hand, and Gabe realized now that the boy seemed to be terrified.

"Uncle Gabe! You've got to help!"

"Jason? What are you doing out here?"

Jason began tugging violently on Gabe's hand. He seemed close to tears.

Quickly, Gabe enfolded the small hand between both of his and squatted down to put himself at Jason's level. "What's wrong, cub? What is it?"

"The men! The bad men are here!"

Gabe saw the boy's trembling, saw the glint of fear in his eyes, and felt himself turn cold.

"The bad men?"

Jason nodded fiercely. He launched into an explanation, but his whispered words ran together in a white heat of desperation.

Gabe's head began to spin. Then Nicky appeared out of the bushes with his little sister in tow. Without a word, the boy drew Gabe back to their hiding place.

Nicky, too, was breathless and excited but, thankfully, more coherent than Jason. With his words shooting out like bullets, he told Gabe their astonishing story, beginning with the arrival of the three men and ending with their capture and detention of Boone.

"You put him *where?*" Gabe gasped with amazement as the recital ended.

"In the fruit cellar," Nicky replied matter-of-factly. "Then we came back here to hide until we could figure out how to get rid of Arno."

"Arno?"

"The man inside with Mrs. Kaine," Nicky reminded him.

Gabe's mind reeled. Still dazed and disoriented from his own earlier ordeal, he found it nearly impossible to take in the boy's incredible tale.

He rubbed a hand over his eyes. "So you told this . . . Boone . . . that *you* hid the notebook. This is the notebook Teddy's supposed to deliver to the federal marshal?"

"Yes, sir. My Papa's notebook."

"Well . . . *did* you? Hide the notebook?" For some reason, Gabe found the boy's apparent calm infuriating.

Nicky met his gaze for an instant, then turned to Jason. "Jason, Sunny's prancing. Maybe you and Stacey had better take her over there beside the tree."

Sure enough, the retriever was circling Jason restlessly, pawing at the snow-covered ground.

"You have to go, Sunny?" Jason queried, as if he expected the dog to answer him.

The retriever stopped and gave a soft whimper, waiting. Quickly, Jason caught Stacey by the hand, and the two of them led Sunny off to the side of the cabin.

As soon as they were out of earshot, Nicky turned back to Gabe. "The notebook is inside Stacey's doll — Mrs. Whispers."

Dumbfounded, Gabe could do nothing but stare at the boy. *"You put the notebook in your sister's doll?"* he finally managed to say.

"*I* didn't," Nicky said evenly. "Papa did.

221

Before . . . they killed him."

In spite of the cold, Gabe felt a wide band of perspiration break out on his forehead. "Stacey doesn't know?"

Nicky looked at him with mild disdain. "Of course not. She doesn't *need* to know. She's as careful with that doll as if it were a real baby. Papa knew where the notebook would be safest."

Gabe shook his head, trying to clear his mind, trying to get a grip on himself. *These people weren't real. . . . Real people didn't live this way. . . .*

His gaze went to the cabin. A figure moved, silhouetted against the window from the glow of an oil lamp, then disappeared from view.

Before Gabe could muster a rational thought, much less a reply to Nicky's remark, Jason and Stacey returned, along with Sunny.

"Mr. Denton?"

Gabe looked at Nicky.

"I think we'd better see about Arno first. Wolf told him if he wasn't back in an hour, Arno was to —" He faltered, looking at Jason. "He was to shoot Mrs. Kaine."

Gabe's throat closed. "Jennifer?" he mouthed softly. "Would he — would he do that?"

The boy nodded solemnly, looking at Gabe as if he were surprised he'd even ask. "Yes, sir. He would. And once Wolf realizes that Teddy lied to him —" He stopped, but his gaze never wavered. "Wolf is crazy. He'll kill anyone who crosses him," he added softly.

"Uncle Gabe?"

Gabe turned to look at Jason.

"Where's Aunt Lyss?"

"She's . . . in the hospital, Jason. There was an accident."

The boy's eyes widened. "Aunt Lyss got hurt?"

Gabe moistened his lips, cracked almost painfully from the cold and the dryness of his fear. "Yes. A truck hit the Cherokee not long after we left. Your Aunt Lyss . . . was badly injured."

Jason's lower lip trembled. "But she'll get better?"

"Yes, of course she will." Gabe couldn't take much more. He felt as if he had been hurled full-force into the middle of a nightmare.

He suddenly became aware of a gentle but persistent tug on his coat sleeve, then on his hand. Glancing down, he met the dark-eyed gaze of a sober-faced Stacey. "Nora says Jesus helps people. I'll ask Jesus to make Jason's Aunt Lyss all well again."

Unable to answer her, Gabe squeezed her hand before he looked away, struggling to gain control of his emotions.

"What are we going to do, Uncle Gabe?" Jason's whisper was choked. "How can we get Daddy and Mommy — and Teddy — away from the bad men?"

Gabe lifted an unsteady hand and glanced around wildly. What should he do? Storm the cabin with three kids and a guide dog? For a moment, he had an almost hysterical urge to laugh. What *should* he do? That was rich. What *could* he do?

"Mr. Denton?"

Nicky's voice was soft, little more than a guarded whisper.

Gabe shot him an impatient glance. The kid had grated on him from the beginning, at first because of what Lyss had called his *precociousness*. Now, however, Gabe looked at Nicky and saw a reflection of Teddy Giordano.

It was unfair. It was immature. It was probably even unchristian. But at this moment, he could barely stand the sight of Nicky Angelini.

His response was curt, even gruff, but the boy simply looked at him with that steady, older-than-time wisdom. His dark, unreadable gaze appeared to register Gabe's anger, even understand it.

"Sir? I think I may have an idea," he said quietly.

TWENTY

When Chuck Arno first heard the moaning, he thought it was the wind. Even when it grew louder and more insistent, he merely thought the storm had picked up again.

It was the dog's barking that made him go to the window and look out. Dogs made him nervous, even more nervous when they barked. He glanced back at the woman. "Is that the guide dog?"

She hesitated, then nodded. "It sounds like Sunny, yes."

"Then Boone must've found the kids." Seeing nothing, he turned, left the window, and returned to stand in front of the woman.

"Oughta teach those kids a lesson, pulling a stunt like that," he growled, watching her.

He didn't like the way she stared back at him. Who did she think she was, anyway? *She* was the one mixed up with a bunch of defects, not him. She needed to be taken down a notch or two, like most women. Once Boone got the kids back inside, he'd settle her dust — teach her how to show a little respect around a real man.

When the dog began to bark even more savagely, he jumped and whipped around. The low moaning sounded closer now, louder.

Arno muttered a curse under his breath as he went to the door that opened onto the deck. The top half of the door was glass, but the louvered shutters were closed. Cautiously, Arno peered through the slats into the black night. The window was fogged, but even when he cleared it, he still couldn't see anything.

The eerie keening started again, louder than before. The dog went on barking.

Arno swallowed hard, glancing back at the woman. She was staring at him with a hollow-eyed, contemptuous look — an expression that made his blood boil.

He opened the opposite shutter, but he still could see nothing except the thick, snow-veiled darkness, a darkness that could hide anything.

It was the sound of his own name drifting in off the wind that finally snapped his control.

"Chuuckk . . ."

He froze. It had to be Boone! He must be hurt.

Suddenly, the barking stopped. There was

nothing but snow-filled silence.

Arno released his breath, at the same time tightening his grip on the gun.

Then it came again. *"Chuuckk . . . help meee. . . ."*

Arno jerked violently, his heart lurching to a stop against his rib cage. He reached for the doorknob, turned it a little, then more. When the lock released, he cracked the door, opening it an inch at a time.

He stood in the doorway, looking and listening. There was nothing. Nothing but darkness and that mind-chilling moaning.

He stepped out, easing over the threshold and onto the deck, the gun extended as he went. He waited, took another step, then stopped.

"Help meee. . . ."

Arno's head whipped to the right, and he choked out a cry of panic as the huge dog came roaring around the side of the cabin at full speed. Its head was low, its mouth open in a furious, snarling rage as it raced toward him. The ground seemed to tilt under him, and Arno felt his bones turn to butter.

The gun in his hand began to shake violently.

Terrified, he screamed as the vicious-looking dog reached the bottom of the steps

— and stopped. Stopped on command.

Before Arno could even catch a breath, a heavy, boot-clad foot came swinging up from somewhere beside him. It cracked his wrist in a painful blow and sent the gun flying across the steps and into the snow-laden bushes.

Arno whirled, raising his arm to strike out. But he was too late. A blond-haired man in a blue ski jacket whacked him with a high kick and a straight-line punch, knocking the wind from him.

He reeled and fell backward, slamming against the wall of the cabin. Again Arno struck out, blindly this time, twisting, kicking, clawing in panic as he wheezed for air.

The man came at him again, and Arno felt his blood turn to ice when he glimpsed the expression of raw fury on the guy's face. He saw the punch coming and scrambled to duck it, but suddenly lights went off in his head, and the night erupted in a blinding white flash.

Two fleeting thoughts knifed through the pain as Arno went down. Out of the corner of his eye, he saw the dog turn and go bolting like a crazy thing, away from the cabin and out into the field, and he felt a stroke of insane relief at its leaving.

Then, seeing the rage on the face of the

man who had attacked him, he wondered if he might not have been safer with the dog.

Jennifer saw most of the scene between Gabe and the thickset mobster through the open door. She watched with dazed astonishment as her brother-in-law efficiently knocked Arno unconscious, then bound his hands with a length of clothesline from the storage pantry.

By the time Gabe, Jason, and the Angelini children came to untie her, she was on the verge of screaming with relief. Instead, she began to sob, losing the last thin shred of her self-control.

She made two or three attempts to pull herself together while Gabe worked on the rope, but once he had freed her hands and feet, she could no longer restrain the effects of the night's terror. Jason threw his arms around her, and the little girl, Stacey, shyly touched her face. Jennifer only cried harder. After a moment, Nicky walked away, going to the other side of the room to stand quietly and watch Jennifer and his sister.

Still on his knees beside her, Gabe tossed the rope aside and clasped her shoulders. "Jenn — are you all right?"

She nodded weakly, wiping her tear-stained face with the back of one hand. "Yes

. . . I'm . . ." She tried to tell him about Daniel, but her lips were trembling so fiercely she couldn't make him understand.

"Jennifer . . . take it easy," he soothed her, still gripping her shoulders firmly. "It's OK now. You're all right."

She shook her head violently and finally forced out the words. *"Daniel!* He's out there with that awful man! Wolf — he took Daniel and Teddy . . . and he has a gun. . . ." Her entire body began to shake as she was once more overcome by the horror of the past few hours.

Jason backed off a little, glancing at his uncle with frightened eyes. Gabe quickly reassured him with a nod, then grasped Jennifer's shoulders even more tightly. "Jenn, I need to go after Dan. You've got to pull yourself together so I can leave the kids with you." He watched her. "Jennifer?"

She nodded, struggling for control. She pulled in deep breaths, hugging her arms tightly to her body. Finally, Gabe dropped his hands away from her shoulders. She squeezed her eyes shut once, hard, then opened them.

Gabe helped her to her feet. "I'm . . . I'm all right," Jennifer assured him, rubbing her wrists where the rope had burned her skin.

Gabe watched her, his expression skeptical. "Sure?"

Again Jennifer nodded. Then, turning to Jason, she exclaimed, "Where *were* you? They said you went out the bedroom window. I was *terrified!*"

"Jennifer." Gabe's voice broke off her questioning, and for the first time Jennifer saw how awful he looked. His face was scratched — or was it cut? There was a small bandage below his ear. His eyes were deeply shadowed and bloodshot. He looked positively stricken.

Suddenly a thought hit her. "Where's Lyss?"

When he didn't answer, Jennifer looked at him more closely. "Gabe? Where's Lyss?"

She caught her breath at the anguish in his eyes. "Lyss is in the hospital. There was an accident . . . not long after we left here."

Too stunned to reply, Jennifer could only stare at him, listening with growing horror as he began to explain.

Would this nightmare never end? The children held hostage . . . Lyss injured . . . Daniel . . .

Daniel!

She turned back to Gabe, but he was already starting toward the door. "Bolt the door behind me," he told her, his voice now steadier, even firm. He actually managed a weak smile. "I'll let the kids fill you in on what *they've* been up to."

"Gabe, be careful. . . ."

"Count on it. You just stay put. Listen, Jenn, I called Giordano's contact people from the hospital. They're snowed in, too, so they couldn't promise me anything. But at least they know where we are, and they'll come when they can." When Jennifer started to question him further, Gabe cut her off. "I also told the hospital to call the police, to send them out here. They'll probably show up anytime now. We're going to be OK."

Jennifer studied him. "Gabe, you know as well as I do that with this storm, there's no telling how long it might be before anyone gets through to us."

"The police will get through," he insisted, not quite meeting her gaze as he again made for the door.

"Mr. Denton?" Nicky Angelini's voice stopped Gabe. He turned, frowning.

"Arno's gun," the boy reminded him. "Shouldn't you take it with you?"

As Jennifer watched, a muscle in Gabe's jaw tightened, and his mouth went hard. "Not everyone settles their problems with a gun," he bit out.

"Gabe, maybe you should take it, just —" Jennifer swallowed her warning at the dark scowl that came over his features.

"I've never had a gun in my hand, and I don't intend to start now. I can take care of that greasy little punk without a gun."

"Would you let me go with you, Mr. Denton?" Nicky pressed. "I know Wolf, how his mind works. . . ."

"Oh, I'll just bet you do, kid," Gabe snapped, his expression ugly. "But I'll take my chances alone, all the same."

The boy looked as if he'd been struck as Gabe whirled around and went out the door, slamming it shut behind him.

After a moment, Jennifer turned to Jason. "Where's Sunny? Is she still outside?"

The boy hesitated. "Sunny went to Daddy," he replied quietly, his face solemn. "I told her to go help Daddy."

Jennifer looked at him, then moved to slide the bolt on the door with a trembling hand, praying with all her heart that Sunny and Gabe wouldn't be too late.

TWENTY-ONE

From his position near the wall of the barn, Daniel heard Wolf's voice thicken with menace.

"You lied to me, didn't you, Teddy?" His tone was soft, but every word was oiled with warning.

Teddy's reply bounded down from overhead. "Hey, man, I was nervous! And it was dark. But I hid it in this hayloft, so it's got to be here."

Listening intently, Daniel could almost feel the electric tension between the two men.

"Oh, you were nervous, were you?" Wolf sneered. "Teddy-boy, I'm disappointed in you. It's not like you don't know better. You worked for Nick long enough to learn *some* smarts, didn't you?"

When Teddy didn't answer, Wolf went on, his words falling quietly off his tongue with a sinister smoothness. "Surely you learned, Teddy. You can't play games with us. Not with the Family."

"I'm not playing games! This *is* where I hid the notebook. It was dark, and I was in a hurry. You're just going to have to give me a little time, that's all." There was an edge of desperation in Teddy's voice, his words shooting out fast and sharp, like jagged pieces of glass.

"Get down here, punk!"

Daniel stiffened at the change in Wolf's tone. The snide, almost playful note of banter was gone, exchanged for a malevolent hiss of anger, an anger that sounded potentially explosive.

"Hey, Wolf, give me a second, will you?" Uneasily, Daniel heard the change in Teddy's voice, too. The brash assurance seemed to have fled, replaced by a distinct note of fear. "Listen, if you'd just take that gun off me, it would help. You're making me so nervous I can't even think. Give me a break."

"Shut up, punk! Just — *shut up!*" The mobster's voice turned shrill. "I'm not wasting any more time with you! We'll let those smart-mouthed Angelini brats dig up the notebook!"

Daniel flinched when he heard a sudden movement from the hayloft. If Teddy panicked and tried to jump this maniac, he wouldn't have a chance.

"Wolf, I told you, the kids don't know where it is! They don't know anything about it. Leave them alone!"

"We'll see, punk. We'll see."

"Wolf, will you be reasonable —"

Daniel heard the click of the gun. He took a cautious step toward Wolf, judging his distance from the mobster to be only a few inches, no more than a yard. "Give him a chance," he said quietly. "You haven't even given him time to look."

"Dan, don't!" Teddy warned.

Ignoring him, Daniel took another step. "Put the gun on me," he said evenly. "Let him look, however long it takes. No man can think with a gun pointed at him."

The only sound in the barn was the rasp of agitated breathing — his own, as well as that of the other two men.

Suddenly Wolf laughed. The brittle, humorless cackle made Daniel feel as if an icy blast of wind had howled through the building.

"What's this?" Wolf jeered, abruptly sobering. "You looking to be a hero, blind man? Huh? You want to play games, too, is that it?"

Suddenly Wolf's arm slammed hard around Daniel's throat in a vicious grip. At the same time, he prodded the gun roughly into his back.

Daniel choked and stumbled, fighting for breath. He sucked in air to ease the pressure on his windpipe.

"Sure, blind man! Have it your way!" Again Wolf laughed. "Hey, punk — your buddy here wants to die in your place! Which one of you wants to go first, huh? You or your pal?"

Daniel tried to think. He had already judged the mobster to be at least a head shorter than him. Even with Wolf's arm around his throat and a gun in his back, if he were quick enough, he thought he could swing forward, roll Wolf over his back, shake the gun free. . . .

Then he heard Teddy shout, heard him move, and suddenly he knew there was no time. Teddy was going to jump.

Daniel twisted, trying to break free of the headlock.

He heard Teddy cry, *"Nooo!"* as he hurled himself from the loft. With one furious surge of strength, Daniel wrenched himself free of Wolf's arm, turned, and threw himself at the mobster. The gun went off, and he heard Teddy utter a small, odd sound of surprise as he hit the ground. At the same instant, the grayness Daniel lived with every day of his life suddenly exploded into a brilliant blaze of flashing colors. He went down, and the light show fizzled and faded to black.

TWENTY-TWO

Through a gray haze of pain, Teddy's eyes began to focus. He saw the golden retriever nuzzle Daniel's shoulder, then begin to lick his face. She whimpered softly a couple of times. Once she looked up, toward the far end of the barn.

When the dog saw that Teddy's eyes were open, she transferred her attention to him, padding over to his side and pulling gently at his coat with her teeth. Teddy lifted a weak hand to the retriever, then, remembering, anxiously scanned their surroundings. There was no sign of Wolf.

He raised himself up from the ground, moaning with the effort. He ran a hand over his arm, then his head and neck, surprised when he found no blood. He hadn't been shot, after all.

He turned to Daniel, pushing himself up to his knees, catching his breath with the effort. His upper left arm was on fire, and something pulled in his back when he moved. But he forced himself to crawl to Daniel. Sunny was beside her master.

Gently, she touched her nose to the side of Daniel's face, but he lay silent and unmoving.

"Dan?"

Quickly, Teddy examined the big man, his gaze locking on the blood seeping from his upper arm. Daniel stirred then, groaning as he opened his eyes. He turned his head slightly, lifting a hand to his throat, then to his shoulder, yanking it away when he touched the wetness on his sleeve.

"Dan . . . just lie still. You took a hit in your arm."

Daniel scowled and uttered another groan of pain. "My shoulder?"

"Yeah. I need to find something to tie it off until we can get you out of here."

"Wolf . . ."

"He's gone."

Sunny began to whimper and lick Daniel's face. He lifted a hand to stroke her ears, then frowned. "Sunny? Where'd you come from, girl?"

The retriever burrowed her nose into the side of his neck for a moment, then sat down beside him, giving Teddy an expectant look.

"Are you all right?" Daniel asked Teddy dully.

"Fine," Teddy replied, studying Daniel.

"Thanks to you. I think I may have a dislocated shoulder and a sprained back, but no bullet holes."

Daniel gave a nod. "I should have a clean handkerchief in my pocket," he mumbled thickly. He pushed himself up enough to get to the pocket of his jeans. "Help me wrap this around my arm, will you?"

Carefully, Teddy helped him free his arm from the sleeve of his jacket, then tied the handkerchief firmly around the wound.

"All right?" he asked, watching Daniel with concern as he helped him back into his coat.

Daniel nodded, propping himself against the wall of the barn.

Teddy searched the other man's face for a long moment. "Why'd you do a crazy thing like that, anyway?" he asked abruptly. "Wolf might have killed you!"

"Instinct," Daniel muttered.

"I don't think so," Teddy said quietly, still watching him. "You meant to save my life."

Daniel tried to smile, but it was more of a grimace. "Had to buy you some time," he said cryptically.

Teddy frowned. "What are you talking about?"

"You don't want to die yet, Teddy,"

Daniel said. "Not until you're ready for heaven." He broke into a spasm of coughing.

Teddy thought the man might be delirious, but a careful look at the expression on Daniel's face indicated otherwise. He swallowed hard but said nothing.

Daniel let his head loll back weakly against the wall, stroking Sunny's ears with his good hand. "We can talk about that later. Right now, we've got to get out of here, get back to the cabin." Suddenly more alert, he leaned forward. "Wolf — that's where he'll go, isn't it? To the cabin?"

"Probably. He thinks the kids have the notebook — or at least know where it is. He'll stop at nothing to get it."

"We have to stop *him*." Daniel started to drag himself to his feet.

"He's still got the gun, Dan." Teddy moved to help him, slumping under the other's weight as Daniel leaned against him.

"But he's coming unglued," Daniel pointed out. "I think the two of us can take him. It will have to be before he gets back to the cabin, though. We might handle one at a time but not all three of them together."

Again Teddy surveyed their surroundings, his gaze stopping on the big red Massey-Ferguson tractor parked in the middle of the barn. He studied it a moment, then turned back to Daniel. "That tractor — does it drive pretty much like a car?"

Daniel considered the question, then nodded. "They're not hard to drive. Not if it's the MF. Gabe said Mac had left it in the barn."

"You think I could drive it?"

"I used to drive one every summer when I worked up here for my uncle. If I could drive it, I'm sure you can. Why?"

"I don't suppose the keys would be in it?"

"The keys?" Daniel shrugged. "Probably are. I doubt if Mac ever worries much about anyone stealing anything out here."

"Even if there are no keys, I can probably hot-wire it," Teddy said, mostly to himself. "Let's go for a ride, Dan."

"Are you sure you're able?"

Not answering, Teddy braced himself to support Daniel's weight, and the two of them moved slowly toward the tractor. Sunny guided Dan on the opposite side. Even without her harness, the retriever herded her master expertly, blocking him from stumbling over a milk can.

"I don't know how far I'd get on foot," Teddy said, thinking out loud. "My back feels like someone's been jumping rope on my spinal cord. But I can still drive. Maybe we can chase Wolf down before he gets to the cabin."

Daniel staggered, then steadied himself against Teddy.

"You all right?" Teddy darted a worried look at him.

Daniel rubbed his throat and nodded, but Teddy didn't like the way he looked. He was pale as a ghost and drenched with perspiration.

They found the keys in the tractor's ignition. "All right!" said Teddy. "Let's go get him." He hoisted himself up to the tractor seat, then gave Dan a hand up.

Daniel settled himself and gave a brief nod to Sunny, who backed off a little, then came at a run, jumping up onto the tractor and squirming into the tight space beside Teddy's foot.

Teddy watched the dog, then turned his attention to the instrument panel. "OK. What do I do first?"

Daniel thought a minute. "Push in your clutch. There should be a switch around the middle of the panel, maybe a little to the left. That's your fuel shutoff switch. Push it in. Then put it in neutral and turn the key."

"That simple, huh?"

"Let's hope."

Teddy rolled his tongue inside his cheek, took a deep breath, and followed Daniel's directions. When he turned the key, he was afraid the engine wasn't going to catch, but after a couple of seconds, the tractor roared to life.

"Whoa," he said with a soft whistle. "How many horses are in this baby?"

"A bunch," Daniel said. "You ready?"

"What now?"

"Put it in gear and give it some fuel. There's a throttle on the floor. Then let your clutch out and go."

"Right," Teddy said under his breath. Finally the tractor lurched, chugged, and moved forward. "Here goes! Has this thing got any lights on it?"

"Below the steering wheel. A little to the right. You've got work lights and flashers. You can run them separately or together."

"I want it all."

"Then turn the switch to the right as far as it will go."

Teddy turned the switch. "All *right!* We've got *lights!* Hey, this is one tough machine. What's that attachment on the back? Looks like some kind of a motor with a metal pipe."

"Must be the PTO — the power takeoff. That's your power machine to drive other equipment," Daniel explained, shifting a little to steady himself. "Mac was probably using it for the grinder-mixer, to grind feed for the cows. You want to stay well away from one of those if it's running," he cautioned. "It'll eat a man alive within seconds."

They left the barn, lights flashing. Teddy was impressed. Then another thought struck him. "Is the snow going to be a problem for us?"

Daniel shook his head. "City boys," he said with a grin. "No, the snow won't be a problem. This is a four-wheel drive. It'll go through just about anything."

"Good thing. We've got some pretty impressive drifts out here."

Even without a moon or stars, there was plenty of light. The snow-covered field caught the glare of the tractor's headlights, illuminating the night around them.

"See anything?" Daniel asked.

Teddy shook his head, then caught himself. "Nothing yet. Hang on, I'm going to turn and head toward the cabin." He was surprised at how easy it was to turn the big machine around and start it in the other direction. They moved slowly around the side of the barn toward the field that led to the main cabin.

Under other circumstances, Teddy thought, he probably would have enjoyed this. He liked to drive — *loved* to drive, in fact — and he had driven just about every kind of machine on wheels. He had even tried a semi a couple of times, but gave it up when he realized he would need a lot more training in order to get the hang of it. He liked the feel of the big Massey-Ferguson under him, its solid strength, the sound of its power. He even got a childish kick out of the flashing lights. *Yeah,* he decided, *this could be kind of fun if it weren't for . . .*

Wolf! The lights caught him a hundred, maybe a hundred and fifty yards ahead, off to the right. Teddy saw the man in the field turn, stopping to stare at the tractor.

"There he is," he said softly to Daniel. "And you were right. He's headed toward the main cabin."

"Does he see us?"

"Oh, yeah," Teddy murmured as he continued to eye the mobster. "But I don't think he was *expecting* us."

Sunny sat up and began to bark.

To Teddy's surprise, Wolf didn't run. He stood like a statue in the snow, watching their approach as if he were too stunned to move.

They closed the distance by several more yards, the tractor roaring like an angry lion over the retriever's frenzied barking.

Then Teddy saw Wolf raise the gun. "Get down, Dan! He's going to shoot!"

Daniel ducked down as best he could, his hand snaking out to hold Sunny. "Watch yourself!" he yelled at Teddy.

Not answering, Teddy continued to grip the wheel, arrowing in on Wolf with fierce determination.

The mobster fired the gun once, then began to run, awkwardly tripping in the deep snow. Teddy gave a grim little smile of satisfaction. It was impossible for the man to make any real headway. The field was layered with one enormous drift after another, and Wolf obviously wasn't wearing boots. Twice he stumbled and went down.

The tractor was closing the distance fast, and Wolf stopped running, again taking time to aim and fire.

"Stay down, Dan!" Teddy shouted without turning to look. "He's close enough to hit us now."

Wolf fired once, missed, and fired again, more wildly than the first time. He shouted something at Teddy, then turned and ran.

Out of the corner of his eye, Teddy saw that Daniel was having a hard time crouching down, and even more difficulty restraining the retriever. Apparently, the combination of the tractor noise and gunshots had agitated the dog. She twisted under Daniel's hand, barking and snarling angrily.

"Sunny, *no!*" Daniel ordered sharply. The dog quieted her barking but continued to pitch feverishly back and forth.

They were closing in on the running man. Teddy could see him clearly now. Without stopping, Wolf pivoted and fired. Seeing that he had missed again, he fired once more, this time stopping for a better aim.

The bullet sailed past Teddy's head, close enough that he could hear it whistle as it went by. But it missed, and he did a mental check on Wolf's ammunition.

Counting the shot that had wounded Daniel, Wolf's gun should be empty. Teddy decided to make sure.

He stood up from the tractor seat and yelled, "Hey, Wolf — want a ride?"

He was close enough to see the mobster's furious expression as he turned and raised the gun. Teddy ducked when the man aimed and fired, but nothing happened. The gun was empty.

With a sharp breath of relief, Teddy lowered himself to the seat. He gripped the wheel, heading straight for the man in the snow.

Wolf threw his useless gun away and began to hurtle as best he could through the snow, looking wildly over his shoulder every few seconds.

"You can get up now, Dan. He's running on empty," Teddy said tersely, his hands glued to the wheel.

Daniel hauled himself up, removing his hand from Sunny's back as he did. Apparently, that was the chance the retriever had been waiting for. She squirmed out of the cramped area, lunged from the tractor, and pounded across the remaining few feet of snow between her and Wolf, barking fiercely as she ran.

"Sunny!" Daniel looked as if he was about to jump after her, and Teddy reached to hold him back, still keeping his eyes on Wolf. "She's all right! Stay put until I stop this thing!" He looked at the panel. "How *do* I stop it, anyway?"

At last Teddy found the brake pedal and brought the tractor to a gradual halt. He took it out of gear but let the motor idle. "Stay here, Dan. I'm going after Wolf!"

Without hesitating, he jumped to the snow-covered ground, ignoring the sudden roar that surged to life behind him. He bolted for Wolf, who was still running as hard as he could.

Sunny beat him there. She charged the mobster, leaped into the air, and hit Wolf's back, a golden fireball of fierce, high-powered fury.

"Way to go, *Sunny!*" Teddy yelled, adding his own weight to the retriever's as he, too, tackled Wolf. The mobster flailed his arms, groping, lashing out at nothing. Then he screamed and went down hard.

TWENTY-THREE

Gabe saw the trio from across the field. Running as fast as he could in his heavy hiking boots, he jumped over a snow-covered tree stump and went on, watching with amazement as Sunny took the mobster down.

He cried out a shout of encouragement to the dog and felt a thrill of grudging relief when he saw Teddy Giordano leap off the tractor to help. He watched Wolf go down, admitting to himself that Teddy was surprisingly good with his punches. One efficient chop, and the mobster's hands stopped grabbing air and fell limply to his sides.

Gabe was only yards away from the scene when he became aware of another noise, a noise that made his stomach constrict with horror — the loud burst of power roaring from the PTO. Someone must have hit the lever.

He stopped dead for an instant, his eyes going to Dan. Somewhere deep inside him a blast of fear exploded. He saw Dan jump from the tractor, then weave unsteadily as his feet hit the ground.

Gabe took off, pushing himself so hard that he was almost flying across the field. The cold stung his face and burned his eyes as he ran. He kept his panic-stricken eyes fixed on Dan, who at first stood unmoving, as if to get his bearings. Suddenly he stepped backward, the movement taking him an inch too close to the rapidly turning, grinding PTO shaft.

Gabe tried to scream, but nothing came out. His chest burned, and his heart banged painfully against his rib cage as he stretched his legs and continued to fly.

Finally he got it out. *"Dan! Don't move! Dan . . . the PTO!"*

Dan froze, but it was too late. Gabe saw the bottom of his jacket touch the uncovered shaft. Over 500 rpms of power grabbed the material and started to wrap the coat.

Gabe's last warning was one long, unbroken scream of sheer terror as he watched Dan throw up a hand to grab something — anything. The movement only made him stumble closer to the PTO. The grinding machine was pulling him into certain death with furious, relentless speed.

With dreadful clarity, Gabe saw that he would never reach his friend in time. Dan cried out, a terrible sound of helplessness.

Gabe pushed himself to the absolute limit. His chest was about to explode, but he was close now, close enough to reach out with both hands to Dan. Then suddenly Teddy Giordano hurled himself at the trapped blind man. The force of his weight ripped Dan free of the PTO with sudden fierceness as Teddy offered himself up to the machine like some kind of pagan sacrifice.

Gabe moved to grab Teddy, but the sleeve of his jacket was too far into the machine to get him free. Throwing himself against the side of the tractor, Gabe hit the lever beside the seat and pushed it back —

It stopped. Stopped just before it would have ground Teddy's arm to the bone.

Even though the tractor was still running, the sudden drop in noise was almost startling as the PTO came to a halt. Sunny, who had deserted the unconscious Wolf to go to Dan, stopped barking.

Gabe killed the motor of the tractor, then ran and dropped down in the snow next to Teddy Giordano, who lay unconscious and bleeding but alive. Gabe pulled off his ski jacket and draped it over Teddy, then started toward Dan.

Shaking, but otherwise all right, Dan had

already hauled himself up from where he had fallen after being knocked free of the PTO. He stood, not moving for a moment as he listened. "Gabe?"

Gabe reached for him, grasping his forearm. "Are you all right?" he choked out, his voice roughened by the fear still lodged in his throat. "You're bleeding."

Dan waved off his concern. "It's nothing." After only an instant's hesitation, the two men embraced each other fiercely.

Dan stepped back, but Gabe still held him at arm's length.

"Teddy?" Dan questioned. "Is he —"

"Unconscious. The shaft caught his arm," Gabe explained. "He's losing a lot of blood." He guided Dan over to Teddy. "We need to get him to a hospital fast, but —"

"*Jennifer!*" Dan suddenly grabbed Gabe's arm, a look of dread settling over his features. "Where is she? Is she all right?"

"Jennifer's fine, buddy," Gabe reassured him. "Everything's under control —" He stopped suddenly. He had to tell Dan about Lyss, but now wasn't the time.

"Thank you, Lord," Dan murmured shakily, raking a hand down his face. "We've got to get an ambulance out here for Teddy," he said urgently. "But how —"

He stopped. Both men stiffened as they

heard a whirring noise.

For a moment neither spoke as the thrumming sound of an engine grew gradually louder.

Gabe looked up. "It's a chopper!" He watched the approaching lights in the night sky above them with excitement. "It must be Teddy's people from Virginia!"

In his relief, he grabbed Dan's injured shoulder, realizing what he had done when Dan grimaced with pain. "Ah, Dan, I'm sorry."

Dan made a weak dismissing motion with his hand. "I'm OK. Do they see us?"

"I can't tell yet."

"Do you think they can land in this much snow?"

"It's heavy enough to be packed pretty solid. The best place would be down by the gate, where I plowed earlier. Stay here," he said. "I'm going to turn on the tractor lights so they can't miss us!"

Teddy's hoarse whisper stopped him. "Gabe?"

Startled, Gabe froze, staring down at him.

Teddy's face was pale and pinched, his eyes barely open. "Thanks, man."

Gabe looked at him, saying nothing. He wasn't angry anymore. He was simply exhausted. Exhausted and sick at heart. He felt nothing for Teddy Giordano. He hadn't the strength to feel anything.

He tore his eyes away from the man on the blood-soaked snow and ran for the tractor. He climbed up, switched on the headlights and flashers, then began to jump up and down, waving his arms and yelling. "Down here! *Hey! Here!* Here we are!"

The helicopter dropped low, hovering long enough for Gabe to see the pilot wave one hand in acknowledgment.

"They see us, Dan!" he shouted. He made a pointing motion with one hand in the direction of the plowed lane leading to the gate.

The chopper came a little lower, circled, and headed in the direction Gabe had indicated.

Putting the MF into gear, Gabe started forward. "I'll be back!" he yelled to Dan. "I'm going down to the gate with the tractor. The lights will help guide them in!"

He bumped across the snow in the tractor, mumbling a hurried prayer of thanks as he went. When he reached the gate, he jumped from the tractor, leaving the lights on full and the engine idling.

The helicopter hovered, veered a little to the right, then began to descend. Gabe continued to pray. He didn't know how much traction one of those things had on snow or ice.

The chopper was down. It landed rough and hard, but safely. Gabe could have wept with relief.

Both the pilot and his passenger jumped from the cockpit and ran toward him.

"Mr. Denton?" a man in a business suit said. "I'm Keith Frye. We talked on the phone." He reached for Gabe's hand and shook it firmly. "Why don't you fill us in on what's happened?"

Gabe's mind reeled, and he groped for words.

"Mr. Denton?" Frye repeated. "Are you able to talk with us, sir?"

Gabe squared his shoulders and took a deep breath. Then, like the professional newscaster that he was, he began a brief, concise, and surprisingly unemotional report of the past few hours' events.

As he drove the tractor back across the field toward Teddy and Dan, Gabe explained how the kids had taken care of Boone, then recited a sketchy account of his own run-in with Arno. He described the scene he had witnessed between Teddy Giordano and Wolf — including how the former had saved Dan's life at the risk of his own. He ended his monologue by revealing the hiding place of Nick Angelini's notebook in Stacey's doll.

"And good luck on getting that doll away from her," he told the marshal with a rueful smile. "You'd better figure out a way to get the notebook out of the doll without . . . *wounding* Mrs. Whispers, or you're going to have a major battle on your hands."

While Keith Frye and the pilot began to work on Teddy, administering first aid and getting him settled onto a stretcher, Gabe told Dan about the accident . . . and Lyss. He tried to be reassuring, answering Dan's questions as fully and optimistically as he could. The whole time, however, he wished he *felt* as confident as he was trying to sound for Dan's benefit.

Once they had loaded Teddy Giordano and the barely conscious Wolf onto the helicopter, Frye headed for the main cabin to check on Jennifer and the kids — and to round up the other two mobsters. Gabe stayed behind, waiting for the backup helicopter the marshal had requested.

The pilot had set flares for the incoming chopper and was now back inside his own aircraft, keeping an eye on Wolf. Gabe stood off by himself, close enough that he could see inside the chopper, where Dan was balanced on his knees beside Teddy

Giordano's stretcher, Sunny nearby. At the moment, Gabe didn't think Dan looked much better than the man on the stretcher. He was pale and perspiring, and obviously in pain whenever he moved his shoulder.

Teddy was conscious, at least enough that he was attempting to carry on a feeble conversation with Dan. His face was pale and pinched, but he clutched Dan's hand as he spoke in a weak, faltering voice.

Gabe didn't especially want to hear anything Teddy Giordano had to say, but he didn't want to let Dan out of his sight, so he stayed put, listening.

"Dan . . . you were right. . . ."

"Right about what, Teddy?" Dan leaned closer to him.

"Both of you . . . you and Gabe. Both of you put your lives . . . on the line for me tonight." He gasped, then choked, "Remember, Dan? I said no one would do that for . . . someone like me." His grip on Dan's hand tightened.

Dan nodded. "But you did the same thing, Teddy — for me. I owe you my life."

Teddy attempted a weak grin. "Yeah, but you're . . . a good man, Daniel. A good man is worth . . . a little pain."

Gabe's eyes burned. Irritably, he wiped the back of his hand across them. The little mobster had that much right, anyway. A man like Dan was worth a *lot* of pain.

Dan's voice was almost as soft as Teddy's when he answered, and Gabe had to strain to hear. "What you have to remember, Teddy, is that in the eyes of God, we're *all* worth a great deal of pain. That's what the Cross was all about." He paused, then went on. "It was God's way of showing each one of us just how very special we are to him. The Cross was for you, too, Teddy. Not just for a few people who measure up. It was for all of us."

Gabe swallowed hard. He suddenly felt certain that Dan knew he was listening, and that his last remark had been meant as much for him as for Teddy Giordano.

It seemed that even blind, Dan could still read his feelings. He had known all along that Gabe resented Teddy Giordano, that the little mobster had grated on him something fierce.

Gabe squeezed his eyes shut, then opened them. Sick at heart, he realized he had forgotten the truth in what Dan had just told Teddy — that the Lord didn't offer his love and forgiveness only to those who measured up. He also offered it to the Teddy Giordanos of the world. The *outsiders*.

Gabe's thoughts suddenly turned to

Nicky Angelini. He remembered with a sick feeling the way the boy had looked at him back at the cabin when Gabe had rejected his offer of help.

He had rejected a *child,* all the while knowing the boy wasn't the problem. His father might have been corrupt, but that didn't mean Nicky was.

The heaviness in his spirit grew as he seemed to hear a voice somewhere deep inside him reminding him that, to God, Teddy Giordano was also a child.

Suffer the children . . . let them come to Me. . . .

Awareness rose slowly at the back of Gabe's mind. Had it not been for Daniel — and Daniel's family — he might have turned out to be a Teddy Giordano or a Nicky Angelini himself.

Or even a Wolf or an Arno . . .

Dan's parents had taken him into their home and their hearts years ago. They had loved him and accepted him and given him a haven from his bitter, alcoholic mother, to whom he had been only an inconvenience. They had taken Gabe to church with their own family week after week for years, teaching him — mostly by example — about the all-inclusive, unconditional love of Jesus Christ. Had the Kaines not . . . *suffered the child,* Gabe might never have become *God's* child.

Overwhelmed by this sudden realization, Gabe watched the two men in the helicopter, straining to hear their conversation.

"Dan, if I come out of this," Teddy Giordano was saying, "I want — I *need* — to talk with you. About . . . some of the stuff I read in Jennifer's Bible." His voice was growing weaker, his eyes fluttering, but he seemed to have Dan's hand in a desperate grip.

Dan bent over him. "We'll talk, Teddy. All you want." He paused. "Besides, there's something I've been wanting to talk with *you* about." A faint smile broke over his haggard features. "I'd like to offer you a job. A job here at the Farm."

Teddy tried to speak but managed nothing more than a choked sound of disbelief.

"You know," Dan went on quietly, "a farm is a great place to raise kids. When you're stronger, we'll talk about that, too. About Stacey and Nicky."

Gabe waited another minute, then climbed up into the helicopter. With tears now spilling from his eyes, clouding his vision, Gabe dropped to his knees beside Dan, studying Teddy Giordano, who was no longer conscious. He touched Dan lightly on the shoulder, then reached for the hand of the man lying on the stretcher.

"Pray for us, Dan," he murmured, as he gripped Teddy's hand. "Pray for him . . . and for me."

EPILOGUE

Helping Hand Farm
August

"The camp has turned out to be even more of a success than you dreamed it would, hasn't it, Daniel?" Jennifer asked quietly.

He nodded contentedly and squeezed her hand. They sat on the porch swing on the deck of the main cabin, enjoying the uncommon quiet of the evening and trying to catch their second wind before vespers. This was their Sunday at the camp. Every third week, Daniel, Jennifer, and Jason drove up to be a part of the Sunday worship and fellowship activities.

"It still doesn't feel right, not having Lyss and Gabe with us on Sundays," Jennifer murmured sadly.

Daniel draped an arm around her shoulders to pull her closer. "Next year," he said confidently. "Next year things will be a little more normal for all of us again. What with the upcoming trial and everything else . . ." Daniel let the sentence trail off, rubbing his arm absentmindedly.

Jennifer noticed the motion and involuntarily shivered at the memory of what might have happened . . . what had *almost* happened. Even after four months, the bullet wound in Daniel's shoulder still gave him a twinge. "It's hard to believe that one little notebook can destroy a criminal ring," she mused. "It's taking a long time to get this trial underway. But I suppose it will be even longer before it's over." She paused. "They *will* go to jail, won't they? The three of them?"

Daniel nodded. "And their boss, I expect. Sabas." They sat in silence for a few more minutes, lulled by the evening's sultry warmth and the sounds of the day gently winding down. They could hear creek water lapping at the rocks along the bank, and the crickets were already tuning up in anticipation of a long summer evening chorus. Every now and then a child laughed or a dog barked, but most of the camp had settled.

Jennifer looked down at Sunny, dozing at Daniel's feet. The retriever's visits were always a treat for Nicky and Stacey, and Jason and the Angelini children had kept her busy most of the afternoon. Now all of them were off with Teddy, helping to collect wood for tonight's bonfire. Apparently Sunny had decided to take advantage of their absence and catch a quick nap.

Jennifer leaned her head against Daniel's shoulder, sighing when he pressed a gentle kiss onto the top of her head. "I'm getting nervous about seeing Lyss tomorrow." She turned to look up at him. "Oh, Daniel — I don't know how she's endured all this surgery!"

His expression betrayed his own concern for his sister. "Hopefully, the worst is over now. Gabe said that from here on, the rest should be easy." He took a deep breath. "Considering the accident, it could have been a lot worse. She could have needed major reconstruction — which would have taken years, not months."

"I only pray this last surgery is a success. She's had bandages on for months, and she's so hopeful," Jennifer said. "I think she's also frightened. But, then, who wouldn't be? If *I'm* this apprehensive about the outcome, what must *Lyss* be feeling?"

"Lyss will be fine. She's said all along that the Lord gave her this face, and he was capable of putting it back together." He shook his head. "That's faith."

"She's been wonderful. She *is* wonderful."

Smiling faintly, Daniel nodded his agreement. "Poor Gabe. When all this first started, he was determined to be so strong for Lyss. *He* was going to get *her* through it, remember?"

Jennifer chuckled. "Lyss told me last week that he's given the word *hover* a whole new meaning."

"I can imagine," Daniel laughed. "When we stopped over there Friday morning, she was threatening to lock him in the garage for the weekend."

Jennifer yawned contentedly. A warm drowsiness crept over her, and she snuggled closer to Daniel. "I think Stacey is really enjoying her birthday," she murmured. "She loved her cornshuck doll. Naturally, she gave me to understand that it would have to share her affections with Mrs. Whispers."

"She's a doll baby herself." Daniel paused. "I hope we'll have a little girl someday. I think I could do a really good job of spoiling a little girl."

"You're already doing a fine job of that with your little boy," Jennifer said dryly. "Nicky and Stacey are both thriving on their new life, aren't they?" she went on, her tone more serious. "I've never seen two happier children. Teddy is just great with them."

"He's great with *all* the kids. Mac told me again today that he doesn't know what he'd do without him. He says Teddy has more energy and works harder than any man he's ever known. And the kids are absolutely crazy about him. Coming from Mac," he added, "that's quite a tribute."

Jennifer nodded to herself. "It's sad that Nicky and Stacey's aunt didn't want to be bothered with them. She doesn't know what she's missing."

"That's true," Daniel agreed, "but I've got a hunch the children are better off. This farm is a great place to grow up, and between the MacGregors and Teddy, they'll have all the love and attention they need."

"Teddy says they should adjust well to school. I'm sure a small rural school will be awfully different for them, especially for Nicky, coming from a private school for the gifted."

"He'll probably be filling in as a substitute teacher in no time," Daniel said with a grin. "Wonder what that boy's going to be when he grows up? A nuclear physicist or a space lab designer?"

"As a matter of fact," a voice said behind them, "he's decided to be a farmer."

"Teddy!" Jennifer jumped, startled. "You're as quiet as a cat!"

"Nicky wants to be a *farmer?*" Daniel asked with unmistakable amusement.

"Yep," Teddy said, coming around the swing to perch on the wide banister. "The entire future of agriculture has new hope."

Teddy had changed, Jennifer thought. His arm had healed without any permanent damage, and he had gained some weight — not too much, but enough to make him look a little healthier.

He looked happy, too. He no longer appeared so tense and *hunted.* Now his eyes held a perpetual twinkle — along with the familiar glint of mischief — and he was seldom without a smile.

"Everything going all right?" Daniel asked him.

"Everything's great," Teddy replied, smiling at Jennifer. "I'll never be able to thank you enough for giving me a chance at this job, Daniel. I like it so much, I almost feel guilty taking a salary for it."

"Well, now, that could be a real problem, Teddy," Daniel said gravely. "Mac's dead set on giving you a raise next month."

Teddy grinned. "I'll either learn to deal with the guilt or give the extra to charity."

It occurred to Jennifer that Teddy Giordano was an extremely likeable fellow. It also occurred to her that he ought to have a nice girl, someone who would appreciate him — and the children.

She would certainly have no problem recommending him to any of the young women in their church family. He was nice-looking, intelligent, amusing, brave. Any man willing to take on two children like Nicky and Stacey as a single parent had to be *extremely* brave, not to mention the way he had saved Daniel's life. That, of course, was what would endear Teddy Giordano to her forever.

On the more practical side, he was a hard worker, and he had a good, steady job. Best of all, he was now an enthusiastic Christian, thanks to Daniel's and Gabe's interest and involvement in his life. Yes, she decided, staring at Teddy with a somewhat conniving smile, she'd definitely have to do some girl-shopping on his behalf.

Teddy looked at her curiously, started to say something, then glanced across the field at the road. "Someone's coming."

Jennifer leaned forward. "That's Gabe's T-bird!" She jumped up from the swing and walked to the end of the deck. "Daniel — I think Lyss is with him!"

Gabe pulled in and parked on the turn-around across from the cabin, then helped Lyss from the car. She was wearing a pink floral sundress and had pulled her hair to one side with a pink silk scarf.

"The bandages! The bandages are off, Daniel!"

"How does she look?" he asked, his voice low and tense.

"I can't tell yet."

Lyss and Gabe came toward them, and Jennifer held her breath. Gabe was smiling — no, not smiling — *beaming*. His face was positively *glowing* with happiness and pride.

Lyss was smiling, too, looking from Daniel to Jennifer. Then she stopped walking and started running. She rushed into Jennifer's arms, and Jennifer held on until Daniel cut in for a big-brother hug.

"You look wonderful!" Jennifer choked out between tears. "Better than we could have possibly hoped!"

Jennifer stood back, holding her sister-in-law at arm's length to study her more carefully. Around her right cheek and ear, hairline scars were still visible, as well as a crescent-shaped scar above her right eye. But Jennifer thought she had never seen a more beautiful sight. It was Lyss — whole and healed and herself again.

"Most of the scars around my hairline will fade," Lyss explained without self-consciousness. "And the stitch marks, too.

It'll never be perfect, but —"

"But then it never was," Daniel jibed. It was the expected big-brother wisecrack, and he smiled when Lyss punched him playfully in the rib cage.

"Aren't you going to look at me, Daniel?" Her expression sobered as she took her brother's hands and placed them on either side of her face.

"You bet I am," he said with a wobbly grin. "We need an objective opinion on this."

His fingertips went over her face in light, deft movements, lingering on the scars as if he longed to heal them. "Well, Pip," he said lightly, his voice none too steady as he completed his inspection, "it seems to me that you're looking good. Real good." He paused. "There's just one thing, though. . . ."

"What, Daniel?"

His index finger lightly traced her nose. "Since you were getting all that work done anyway, I'm surprised you didn't go ahead and get a nose job while you were at it."

Lyss laughed. "Ah, yes, the Kaine nose. I always said I'd get it fixed, didn't I?" She paused and winked at Jennifer. "But I wasn't sure I'd recognize myself when I came out of all this," she went on. "I figured I should keep my most prominent landmark intact."

Jennifer grinned. "I've always liked the Kaine nose. It gives your face — and Daniel's — a kind of strength."

"In Dan's case, a *great* deal of strength," Gabe said gleefully.

Before Daniel could retaliate, Jason came running up with the Angelini children and Teddy Giordano. Lyss hugged everyone, including a suddenly shy Teddy.

"Gabe, would you get that package out of the trunk for me, please?" Lyss asked, turning to her husband.

"That's the *real* reason I wanted to come today," she explained as Gabe went back to the car. Her gaze went to Stacey, who was staring up at Lyss with solemn, awe-filled eyes.

"We have a very special delivery to make," Lyss went on. "I was told that today is someone's birthday." Stacey bobbed her head up and down excitedly.

Gabe returned with the package, and Lyss placed the long, brightly wrapped box in the little girl's arms. "This is for you, Stacey." She paused, then added softly, "Just for you. With my love."

With dancing eyes, Stacey dropped down on the ground to open the gift. "Oohhh!"

she breathed as she carefully lifted from the wrapping a brand-new, curly maple fiddle with its bow.

She studied it lovingly for a long moment before turning her gaze on Lyss and then Gabe. "My very own fiddle?"

"Truly your own, dumpling," Gabe answered. "Lyss made it just for you."

"I've never made a fiddle before, Stacey. Only dulcimers. I hope it turns out to be a good one."

The little girl clutched the fiddle to her heart as if it were a rare and precious treasure. She looked up then and said, with great dignity, "It's the most perfect fiddle in the world. It's even more better than Uncle Gabe's."

At that, Gabe smiled and dug down in his pants pocket to pull out a small package wrapped in plain brown paper. He looked at Nicky, then handed him the package.

"Nicky? I know it's not your birthday," he said quietly, "but I asked Lyss to make something for you, too. Something . . . special." He looked the boy squarely in the eye and added, "After all, you're an adopted member of our family now."

Wide-eyed, Nicky hesitated, then took the package. "May I open it now, Mr. Denton?" he asked, obviously trying to restrain his enthusiasm.

"Please do," Gabe said dryly.

Jennifer saw her brother-in-law's suppressed smile, and she watched, curious, as Nicky slowly and methodically removed the wrapping and opened the lid of a small, delicately carved wooden box.

The boy caught a sharp breath. He looked up at Gabe in disbelief for a long time before returning his gaze to the box in his hand. With great care, he lifted from the box an exquisitely carved wooden replica of a golden retriever. The figurine looked exactly like Sunny.

Gabe cleared his throat awkwardly. "Did you see the inscription on the box lid?"

Nicky looked at him, glanced down at the box, then read aloud in a faltering voice:

"For Nicky Angelini: Because I owe him." Nicky swallowed hard, then added, "It's signed . . . *Gabe.*"

Nicky stared up at Gabe with a stunned expression. After a long silence, he extended his hand. "I — I don't know what to say, sir."

"How about, 'Thank you, Uncle Gabe'?" A corner of Gabe's mouth quirked. Then he grinned and took Nicky's hand. "I'm getting a little tired of *sir.*"

Jennifer held her breath as she watched. After all that had happened, she knew this was difficult for both of them.

Nicky stared at Gabe for another few seconds. Suddenly, in what Jennifer was certain must have been the first impulsive gesture of this strange little man-child's life, the boy moved in and hugged Gabe tightly around the waist. Gabe's face creased with pleasure as he wrapped Nicky in his arms, releasing him only when Lyss put her arms around both of them.

"Hey! How about a hug for the whittler?"

Laughing, Nicky threw his arms around her and thanked her. Not about to be left out of this display of affection, Stacey jumped up and joined her brother in Lyss's arms.

Gabe stooped and whispered something to the Angelini children. They turned, glanced over at Jennifer and Daniel, and came toward them, carrying their gifts.

Stacey looked up at Daniel, then very carefully took one of his large hands and placed it on her precious new fiddle.

"Here, Uncle Dan — do you want to look at my fiddle?"

"And my retriever, too," Nicky added, smiling at Jennifer.

His expression solemn, Daniel took the

fiddle and went over it with careful hands. Shifting it under one arm, he then took the small wooden figurine from Nicky and examined it.

"These are absolutely beautiful," he said as he returned the children's treasures. "But I'm not surprised. Lyss has always had her own unique way of taking something that might not look like much to anyone else and turning it into something really special."

He paused, a fleeting look of wry amusement scurrying across his features as he shot a grin in Gabe's direction. "Of course, at times," he added, "she's had her work cut out for her. But even then I'd have to say she's managed to work wonders."